M000166182

ISBN:978-1-952101-80-9

 Created with Vellum

Bosson NOTICE

THE LORD BROTHERS OF MANHATTAN

ZOEY LOCKE
Z.L. ARKADIE

CHAPTER 1
Off The Clock
DELILAH O'SHAY

Ding, ding, dum, dum...
I awaken with a gasp, then blink into focus my ringing cell phone.

"Oh..." I massage my temples. My head, which feels like the consistency of cement, sinks deeper into my pillow. Last night I hung out with my favorite cousin, Xena, and friends I haven't seen in forever. We danced. We drank. We danced some more. I had a good time—my dull, throbbing headache is evidence of that.

But lying here in my very comfortable bed, I know something is wrong. I'm not supposed to be still in bed. There's too much light in my room. I was supposed to wake up extra early this morning to get to the office and do something.

What was it?

What time is it?

The phone is on its fourth chime. It'll do eight before sending the caller to voice mail. I squint at the screen.

"Damn it," I breathe.

It's Orion Lord, my boss. The time at the top of the screen glares back at me.

I wince as I fling myself up and into the sitting position. It's 11:00 a.m. I had planned to be at the office three hours ago—and now I remember.

The letter.

My heart constricts as I panic. But then, I also remember that Orion never gets in before noon on Fridays. So, I have nothing to fear.

Feeling a teensy bit more relaxed by the seventh chime, I snatch my cell phone off the nightstand as I spring to my feet. "Good morning, Orion." I sound extra chipper to make him believe I'm at my desk working my ass off.

"I've been calling you all night and this morning." His tone suggests I had committed an unholy act by not answering when he called. I had definitely done something unusual by avoiding his after-hours disturbances. Yesterday afternoon, I let Xena persuade me to put my cell phone in Do Not

Disturb mode and leave the office before 5:00 p.m. I unsilenced my device before bed but forgot to set my alarm. And now, I can't chance him making it to the office before I do.

"Mm-hmm. Well, you found me now." I laugh a little too high and then freeze midmotion. "Where are you?"

Orion never pauses for this long. He's the sort of man who presents with an annoying kind of confidence. It's as if he never has to think about what to say or do because he thinks second-guessing himself is a weakness. And so that pause means something is definitely amiss. I leap out of bed and move fast.

"On my way into the office," he finally says.

I speed-walk to my closet, an actual walk-in closet in New York City. I can afford it because Lord Technical Innovations pays me an executive's salary to be the assistant to one of the world's worst executives. The money is why I never complain about him to his face, even when he assigns me the silliest tasks.

"Okay!" I say cheerily as I peel a navy blue shift dress off the hanger. "I'll see you soon."

I wait for him to say something. Orion's not one of those people who ends a call without a *goodbye* or a *see you soon* or a *thank you*. Even though he's a horrible and annoying boss, he has fantastic manners and persuasive charm.

"By the way, you didn't send me my calendar yesterday," he says.

If I had the time, I would stop dead in my tracks, but I don't have the time so I shove my feet into my running shoes as fast as I can. "I know. Sorry. The power went out at around four thirty."

"Which is why I was calling you."

I shove three pieces of gum in my mouth since I can't brush my teeth because he would hear me if I did. "I know… Sorry." *Not sorry.*

"Don't worry. I got it."

Now I go rigid in the middle of hanging my satchel over my shoulder. "You did?"

No…

Please, God, no.

"Yes," he says.

I can't afford to stand still while staving off my second panic attack of the morning. I'll probably have more before the day is over. Orion only knows how to access his calendar through my computer. *No…* I'm stabbing the Down button to the elevator with my elbow while staring longingly in the direction of my apartment. I feel like I've forgotten something.

"How?" I close my eyes, chastising myself for asking that question. I didn't mean to say it that way. Orion may be superficial, but he's not dense. On very rare occasions he'll shock me by displaying moments of brilliance. However, he's never been able to access his calendar remotely. Let's just say that I have a sneaky feeling he pretends not to know how to access his calendar remotely. Regardless, after I tried to walk him through the process dozens of times, he threw up his hands and insisted that I push his calendar to his devices three times a day throughout the workday and on weekends if something changes. Something is constantly changing on the weekends.

For instance, Heather, his date for his brother's wedding this weekend, for which the festivities start today, had called and told him to find someone else to go with. She was angry because Orion hadn't answered any of her thirtysomething messages and eleven emails. I so desperately wanted to let her know that ghosting women he makes dates with is his MO. I have no idea why he does it, but I think it's psychological or psychotic or something in between. But I've come to know Heather well. She was bluffing, which is why I never passed on her message.

However, he has paused again, and now my insides are sending SOS signals to my feet. He couldn't have gone back to the office yesterday evening, could he? No way. He never returns to the office after he leaves. But I had turned my phone off. *Oh no.* I clutch my chest as the elevator stops on the eleventh floor. I know I should've run down the stairs instead of getting myself trapped in the slow-est-moving elevator in New York City. I don't have enough patience to stop. I need to keep going, especially if...

Oh no...

"I figured it out," Orion finally says.

A guy with curly black hair, the most gorgeous eyes I've ever seen, the body of a marble master-piece, and perfectly white teeth smiles coyly at me as he joins me in the elevator. This isn't our first time smiling at each other this way as we say good morning or good afternoon and on rare occasions good night. Once, he said good night to me while wearing a beautiful woman, who appeared to be a supermodel, draped over his shoulder. He's always flirting though. But I'm certain I'm not his type. I never have the time to make myself look like his type. Just like this morning, as I left the house wearing no makeup. *Shit.* I pat the side of my head, remembering I left my apartment so fast that I had forgotten to neaten my ponytail.

So, realizing that I look a mess, I shy away from smiling back at Mr. Eleventh Floor, which is what I call him in my head and when I talk to Xena and my girlfriends about him.

"You figured it out?" I try to whisper to Orion while staring in the opposite direction of Mr. Eleventh Floor. He smells extraordinary today. I love a man who smells like heaven.

"Yes, I did," Orion replies.

"But how?"

"Well, I'm not an idiot, Lilly," he says and then explains some obscure process he used to access his calendar.

If I weren't in such a rush, I would accuse him of purposely trying to confuse me. He does that sometimes.

I jump when the elevator dings. Dang it, I should've muted our call before the car stopped.

"Where are you?" Orion asks.

I race into the lobby. "I just got coffee."

He pauses yet again. "Oh yeah. On the fourth floor or at Starbucks?"

"Starbucks."

"The one around the corner?" he asks.

"Yep!" I sound extra chipper.

"Did you get me one too?"

My lungs burn as I practically run up Fourteenth Street. "Yep, black, no sugar or cream."

"Are you running?" he asks.

"Yep."

"Why?"

"I have a lot of work to do, just trying to get back as fast as I can," I say, trying to control my breaths.

"That's great. You're great, Lilly." He sounds patronizing, and I wonder why.

I frown as I narrowly avoid slamming into a pedestrian who's following the normal New York City sidewalk-walking speed, which is very brisk and at a steady pace. But did he just call me *Lilly* again? He never calls me Lilly. He always calls me Lila—and nobody calls me that but him—even though I've told him more times than I can remember that nobody but him calls me that, but he still does it just to annoy me. But now he's calling me Lilly? *What's he playing at?*

"Right," I barely say.

"You don't believe me?"

I want to huff and puff, but I can't tip him off that I'm running. However, even though I can't see his face, I can very well picture his charming smile. Orion can charm cheese from a starving mouse. But there's no black or white answer to the question he just asked. He's being manipulatively charming and I have no idea why, although my brain has propelled me into figure-out-why mode.

Has he read the letter?

I picture myself sitting at my desk yesterday, before the power went out, grumbling to Xena about what had happened that morning. Orion woke me up with a phone call at 7:03 a.m. and asked if I could bring him a bottle of cold water and towel. He was in the neighborhood, jogging on the High Line. I had dragged myself out of bed, grabbed a fresh bottle of cold water out of my refrigerator, and a towel from my hallway cabinet and met him on the corner of Ninth Avenue and Fourteenth Street. Orion showed no signs of ever breaking a sweat. He claimed he went for a run, but I thought it was more like a walk, and not even a power walk. He grinned at me with that annoying twinkle in his eyes as if I should've felt blessed to be doing him a favor. *He's such a narcissist.*

He didn't even say thank you either. He just

gobbled down the bottle's contents as though he had spent the morning in hell and finally had been given ice water. But I didn't care. All I wanted to do was turn my back on him and pretend our strange encounter never happened. Yet before I could spin around on my heels and stomp back to my apartment, he said, "Wait a minute. I'll give you your towel back." Then he proceeded to wipe his nonexistent sweat.

I glared at him, asking myself, *What do women see in him?* On a subconscious level, I'm aware that Orion Lord is an extremely handsome man. But frankly, I cannot allow myself to acknowledge his looks. The way he behaves doesn't allow me to see them.

"Whoa," he finally said. "You don't look so good. Did you get enough sleep last night? Because you can't take off today. I need you." To drive the point home, he aimed his half-drained water bottle at me. "I need you."

My mind experienced some sort of mental traffic jam full of insults, expletives, and explanations. For instance, "Yeah, I look like crap because I was stuck at the office until 2:00 a.m., finishing a report for your brother Hercules's office that was supposed to be completed by you." *By the way, I do his work too.* I also wanted to say, "When was the last time I had a day off?" I can never take off. If I did, the whole office would go to shit.

But instead, we stood at the bend of the street corner, cars whipping by way too fast, people whipping by even faster, as he kept talking and talking, *and yapping.* I tuned him out as the words *I think I hate you* repeated in my head. The guy didn't even look at me while he talked. His eyes kept wandering to all the beautiful women who were out and about. I think he's a sex addict or something. The guy juggles so many women and cares for none of them. That's why I was surprised that he was so jealous when he learned his brother Achilles was engaged to Treasure Grove, who is apparently his ex-girlfriend. Last year, on top of all the important work I do for him on a daily basis, he made me befriend Achilles's assistant, Jenn, so that I could easily track his brother and his brother's fiancée's whereabouts.

Finally, Achilles and Treasure are getting married in Las Vegas this weekend. They rented out an entire hotel, which costs the same amount as it does to run a small country. I think their soon-to-be nuptials is one reason why Orion has been acting so needy. I almost feel sorry for the guy, almost.

"Recycle this, Lila," he had said, shoving both towel and bottle into my chest.

I was ready to claw his perfect face off. I almost said, "You narcissistic nitwit, do not call me Lila. How many times do I have to tell you not to call me that!"

But I didn't. Instead, I turned my back on him and stormed home, licking my wounds the whole way. However, it was on that walk when a solution to rid myself of Orion Lord for good began to spark in my brain.

"You still there?" he asks.

I thank the Lord I don't live far from the office. I peer through the window of Starbucks and see a line that feels as long as the entire East Coast. It's 11:11 a.m., I can't believe Starbucks is still crowded.

"Oops," I say. "I dropped the coffees." I tell him I'll make some more once I'm back in the office.

"You never answered my question," Orion says.

He made me lie about the coffees and now I have to lie again. *Grrr...* "Yes. I believe you," I say through the fake smile I conjured just to get those words out.

I finally race into the LTI building.

"Why are you breathing so heavily, Lilly?"

I am breathing heavily. Sweat warms my fore-head and trickles down the sides of my face. Our office is on the first floor. We used to be on the pent-house floor with Hercules, and his co-CEO and wife, Paisley, until Orion screwed that up. Then his job duties changed and we were moved to the sixteenth floor to join the sales team. He screwed up there too, and now we're crunching numbers in an office with two rooms—both the same size—but still Orion insists that we share the same space while the other room be used for storing paper, pens, books, ledgers, a copier-printer-fax machine combo, and a refrigerator. He could have his own office and I could have mine. But rarely do any of Orion's decisions make sense.

"Lilly, are you still with me?" he asks.

I scan my employee badge to enter our private hallway. "I'm breathing heavily because I want to hurry up and get to my desk." I squeeze my eyes shut, shaking my head. "I mean back to my desk."

I pull up to a stop when I notice the office door is cracked open. Oh no, did I forget to close it before leaving in a huff yesterday afternoon? I take a moment to visualize myself walking out into the hallway. I was definitely hopped up on a high dose of fuck it. But I don't have to think about what happened yesterday anymore. I know he's in there —I can feel him in the air.

My stomach lurches as I cross the threshold of the office. I'm now existing in slow motion as I lock eyes with Orion who's sitting behind his desk, fingers behind his head and long legs crossed on his desk as he nails me with the cockiest grin.

He points his fingers at me as if he's aiming a gun. "I bet you thought I'd be on my way to the wedding."

I can feel my eyebrows hovering just above my eyes. "I didn't." He and Heather are supposed to board his private airplane at eight p.m. I set my bag on top of my desk, peering at my computer. "What are you doing here so early?"

Oh no. I stifle a gasp. My screen is up. The last task I worked on populates the screen. My head feels floaty as I pretend not to be bothered by the letter that's on display and waiting for anyone and everyone to see. *Has he read this?*

Dear Orion Lord, (You fucking narcissist—remember to delete)

A day comes when an overqualified assistant becomes tired of picking up your laundry, managing your many girlfriends, lying to them, acting as your personal alarm clock, and a new low, even for you, Mr. Lord, bringing you a cold bottle of water at the end of your run. You run? When did you start running?

Never mind.

Oh…I almost forgot, having me stalk your brother and his fiancée was not your finest moment and is actually lower than the water thing. (Delete—maybe.)

The point is, yes, the money is excellent, but you are not (Remember to revise). I quit. This is my two weeks' notice.

Not Even Sincerely, (Remember to delete)
Delilah O'Shay

My eyes flick up and rest on his face. He's still grinning.

I point at my iMac. "Did you see this?" I figure I might as well just come right out and ask.

Orion's eyebrows furrow as he promptly wipes that smug smile off his face. "Read what?"

Hmm…maybe he hasn't read it.

I sit down fast and save my two weeks' notice in a personal and locked folder. "What's on my desktop."

He's on his feet, moving in my direction. "What's on your desktop?"

I slyly click my mouse to collapse the document.

"Nothing." I frown, irritated by the way he's hovering over my shoulder. Also, I don't know if I believe him. Orion reading my two weeks' notice sort of explains his "You're so great, Lilly" comment. He's trying to butter me up because he needs me.

I twist my neck to look up and then scrutinize every lift, wrinkle, and pull of his facial expression. If he had read my two weeks' notice, then he has an expert poker face. I've never known Orion to care enough to withhold his thoughts. He believes everybody wants to know exactly what he's thinking or feeling simply because he's the great Orion Lord. But his long legs are like stalwart tree trunks, blocking me from getting away from him. And I swear his crotch is only a few inches away from the tip of my nose. I'm tapping down a panic attack, a real-life panic attack. He's blocking me in. I'll never be able to get away from him.

"Listen," he says.

"Could you…" I breathlessly say at the same time.

"I need you to go to Vegas with me this weekend." Of course, he takes the floor, making my jaw drop.

Then I recall the one reason why he isn't in

Vegas right now. Yesterday before he left early, he sent Achilles bunk numbers for the week, which in turn made Achilles warn him not to show up at the wedding until the reports were accurate. He had fucked up my beautiful error-free report on purpose. I wanted to chop his head off.

"Then you sent Achilles my error-free report," I say.

Finally, he puts space between us. "I knew that bothered you," he says as though he just solved a grand mystery.

"Well, yes, Orion."

He's on his way back to his desk.

"I spent two weeks working on that report. I put a lot of effort into it just for you to screw it up in one sitting." Gosh, I'm brazen this morning. I've never been this way with him to his face and I like it.

Orion plops down in his chair and squints at his expensive watch. "Listen, I need you in Vegas with me this weekend. We'll need to leave soon."

"Me?"

"Yes, you."

"What about Heather?"

He stops admiring his watch. "She's not coming."

My face contorts into several expressions as I try to process how to respond to his latest demand. *You can go to hell* might be too harsh at the moment. Maybe in two weeks it'll be the perfect thing to tell him. Unfortunately, I still need him for a final paycheck. However, the short answer is *no, Orion Lord. I will not go to Las Vegas with you. I don't want to be anywhere near you during my weekend off.* But then a small voice in my head asks why. Orion, why are you asking me to go to your brother's wedding with you? It's odd, very odd. He has a million women, women, who would jump at the chance to be his wedding date.

I stare at my computer screen. If only it could talk and tell me if he had indeed snooped and read my notice.

"I'll pay you triple your salary," he blurts as if he's strategically sweetening the deal. "And we're flying private. You'll have your own room in a luxury hotel." He smirks naughtily. "Far away from me if you prefer. And all of your expenses are to be paid."

Far away from him? Why would he say that? I turn my head slightly to eye him suspiciously. "Are you sure you didn't see what was on my screen?"

He chuckles. "Why do you keep asking me that,

Lila? Is there something you're hiding?" One corner of his mouth rises into a devilish smirk. "Are you skimming off the top?" He laughs softly. "After all, I give you a lot of access to my accounts, more access than I give anyone else." He seems as though he's about to say something else, but then he presses his lips and rubs his chin.

Well, at least he's back to calling me Lila, which is a mild relief. But still, I can't stop shaking my head. "But why do you want to pay me to go to Vegas with you? I'm sure there is a line of beautiful women who will jump at the chance to go with you."

His smirk intensifies. "And you wouldn't get in line?"

I shake my head rapidly. "Not really." *Hell no is more like it.*

He's stroking his chin again. "Why is that, Lila? You don't think I'm a catch?"

Did he really ask me that question?

"There's that face again," he says.

I even out my expression. "What face?"

"The stink face."

Oh…that face. "I don't have a stink face."

"Yes, you do. But never mind that. I need a platonic date. Someone who looks at me the way you do. No pressure. We get through the weekend. I'm not alone. All business. And as I said, I'll pay you very well."

I should say no and tell him that I'm going to quit. But I can use the extra money. Also, an all-inclusive weekend trip to Las Vegas without being his "real" date isn't so bad. I could use a mini break, and if anybody owes me one it's him. I won't be his obedient, closed-mouth assistant this weekend either. If he sucks, then I'll tell him he sucks. That's what I should do before I eventually quit—one whole weekend of telling him the truth, no holding back.

"Okay," I say, puffing up my chest and folding my arms across it. "I'll be your whatever for the wedding." I won't call myself his date. I will never be his date.

CHAPTER 2

Mr. Eleventh Floor

DELILAH O'SHAY

I suggest he stay while I go to my apartment. It will take no more than half an hour to pack a suitcase and make it back to the office. But Orion insists on driving me to my building where he'll wait.

"We have one hour, Lila." He taps the face of his watch. "Time is essential."

I stop myself from blurting a cynical laugh. Is he serious? The man who is never on time for anything is claiming the essentiality of time? As the British say, bollocks!

It's pure torture being alone with Orion in his ultra-posh luxury car. I think it's a Mercedes or a BMW. It could be a Rolls Royce. I don't know. I have no knowledge of cars whatsoever. But what he drives is very nice. I never thought I'd ride in a car like this in my life. Even though we share the same office space, I don't think we've ever swapped air this close in proximity for such a prolonged period of time, which has been all of one minute. I sit very still, feeling like if I glance in his direction, I'll break into pieces. I was right to presume that Orion already knows where I live. He's making all the right turns to get to my building without me directing him. *What has he been doing, following me?*

"So…" he starts as though he's about to address an old friend. "Why did you turn your phone off last night?"

I stop myself from saying something like, "What? It was off?" Or, "The power drained from my device." Instead, I shift uncomfortably in my seat because for once when the pressure is on, I don't want to retreat. The truth sits on the tip of my tongue and I want to say it. "Because I didn't want to be disturbed."

He does a double take of me. "If you had your phone on last night then we wouldn't have to rush today."

Say it, Lilly, I urge myself. *Say it.* Instead, I turn to see the face of the person who just expertly gaslit me. Grinning, he's so full of himself as he makes the final turn and stops the car in front of the lobby, and just in time for some guy to crane his neck to admire the car.

He catches my gaze on him and then lowers his brows as if my facial expression disturbs him. If only I could see what he sees. My mouth is agape and my lips are quivering. I want to accuse him of gaslighting me yet again. The accusation is stuck on the tip of my tongue. The way I feel is not healthy —he is not healthy.

Finally, he rips his gaze off me, apparently choosing not to ask me whatever he's thinking, and scowls at his expensive watch. "You have fifteen minutes."

Every fiber of my being is telling me to flip him the bird and shout, "I change my mind you narcissistic nitwit. Oh, and by the way, I quit!" But instead, I quickly do the math. I live in an expensive city. My rent is very steep and the only reason I get a break on it is because I work for LTI, who pays 30 percent of rent for all of their high-level executives. Of course, I'm just an executive assistant, but Hercules is the one who interviewed me for my job four and a half years ago. He warned me that being his brother's assistant would be no walk in the park, however, I would be compensated handsomely for my work by receiving an executive-level salary and perks. He then gave me ample opportunity to get up and walk out the door. But I didn't go. The time got away from us as I told him why I had to stay and deal with his difficult brother. After all, I had a BA in psychology, graduating magna cum laude. I didn't tell him I was also a trained dancer, who had satisfied the graduating from college aspect of my life merely to please my parents.

However, I told Hercules about my father's car accident, which five years to the month of my interview had left him paralyzed. Then, one morning my dad woke up and could wiggle his toes. Our family entered him into a very effective but expensive physical rehabilitation program. So, the bills mounted quickly. That's why I needed the money. That's why I would figure out how to make it work with his difficult brother. To date, my dad's treatment has been worth every red cent. He's able to walk on his own again and soon, Dr. Willis says, he'll be able to run too. I figure, all I need is to bank at least six months of the amount I pay for my dad's physical therapy. This weekend will put me over the top, which will allow me to say sayonara to Orion after two weeks from Monday.

I calm myself with that thought as I smile at his

overly handsome face. He's the last man in the world who deserves to be so good-looking.

"Okay," I sing overenthusiastically. "Fifteen minutes it is." I can acquiesce to him because I'm leaving him, and soon, he'll have to do all of his own work or end up in the basement—his choice. He'll fail. And I wish I could get a front-row view of him languishing in the basement with his new shitty assistant as he continues to be a loser.

IT TAKES LESS THAN TEN MINUTES TO PACK MY underwear, two party dresses, one summer dress, my favorite nightshirt, and beauty and hygiene essentials. I brush my teeth with my electric toothbrush and then pack it too. I grab my laptop, thinking this weekend will afford me the perfect opportunity to craft a more civil letter of resignation.

"No laptop," Orion says as he puts my suitcase in his trunk.

My brain scrambles like dice being shaken in a cup as I see the most important task I plan to complete this weekend being ripped away from me. "What?"

"No laptop."

With my jaw dropped, I can't stop staring at him, wondering what in the world has gotten into him. The Orion I know wouldn't care if I brought my laptop or not. And what's he going to do if I insist on taking it with me? Fire me? I have one and a half feet out the door already. My lips stutter as I'm just about to say those beautiful two words for real this time—"I quit." For a split second, I visualize myself tugging my suitcase out of the trunk with a resounding, "Go to hell, boss from hell." *But the money...* "Fine," I grumble, and run my laptop back up to my apartment.

On the way down, the elevator stops on the eleventh floor and in walks the man himself, Mr. Eleventh Floor. This guy is so gorgeous. His looks are a mashup of the hot jock next door and a depiction of a sexy brooding vampire. He can't be that much older than thirty. I only guess that because of the graceful way he carries himself. His face has that eternal youthful quality to it. But I've never seen him this way before. He's flustered and he wears it so sexily.

His eyes immediately widen with recognition. "What a coincidence."

"And this time, I didn't even make a plan to run into you," I say with a laugh.

His thick and naturally manicured eyebrows shoot up. I think he's actually pondering whether or not I'm a stalker.

"That was a joke," I say. "And obviously a bad one."

We chuckle to let the awkwardness pass. I can't believe I said that.

Mr. Eleventh Floor tells me he had to return to his apartment because he had left his cell phone sitting on top of the sofa.

"That sounds totally like something I'll never do," I say with a laugh.

Thankfully, he chuckles too. "Me neither. I'm exhausted and I won't be able to slow down until this weekend is over."

Pinching the bridge of his nose, he tells me he's been up all-night watching player performance videos.

"I'm usually a laid-back kind of guy but when the season starts, I turn into a rabid workaholic. I gotta win the big one."

Gosh, I love the shade and shape of his eyes. Even better are his kissable lips, which actually resemble Mr. Boss from Hell, Orion Lord's. But Mr. Eleventh Floor is much dreamier because he's clearly not a selfish asshole, and he's athletically tall too. I'm sure he has a girlfriend. Men who look like him are never single. That would also explain why he hasn't taken our encounters further than casual convo.

"What's the big one?" I ask as the elevator stops on the fifth floor to let someone else in. It's a woman. Her perfume is nice. But I don't acknowledge her because he doesn't, which might be a sign that he's into me. *Hmm…*

"The World Series."

"Oh," I exclaim, leaning away from him. "Baseball?"

"The Connecticut Ramblers." He's watching me with a perfect toothy white smile. *Gay…he must be gay.*

"Wait? The Connecticut Ramblers?" I ask.

"Yep." He looks pretty proud about whatever association he has with that team. I wonder if he's the coach or something.

The doors slide open, and as we pass through the lobby, I share with him that I'm attending the wedding of the team owner's sister this weekend.

He pulls his gorgeous mouth downward reflectively. "Oh yeah? Will you be with the bride or groom?"

"Both," I say. "The groom's brother is my boss, but I'm friendly with the bride." I'd rather claim her than him. I would think Treasure and I would remain friendly long after I leave LTI. She's the epitome of a girl's girl.

An impish smile forms on his lips. "Treasure, huh?" Of course, he knows her. He would know the owner of the team's sister's name. She's pretty popular as she's been nicknamed "The People's Heiress." Treasure always gets a kick out of that.

I jump startled when a loud horn echoes through the hollowed-out open space of the porte cochere. Mr. Eleventh Floor remains calm, cool, and collected as he watches my crazy boss standing at the driver's side of his car yelling, "Lila, let's go."

I bite down on my back teeth. *I will not allow him to call me Lila from this day forth.*

I'm about to excuse myself and apologize for my boss's behavior, but Mr. Eleventh Floor is frowning at Orion. "Is that Orion Lord?"

Surprised he asked, and alarmed that he knows the boss from hell, I spread my fingers against my breastbone. "Yes." My tone is laced with caution.

Suddenly Orion jerks his head back. "Lynx is that you?"

No...no-no-no-no. Please don't let them know each other.

The two are suddenly grabbing each other's hand and shaking hands in that manly way followed by a loose hug.

No...

I sigh with dread. *Yes.* All my hopes of getting to know Mr. Eleventh Floor better are immediately thwarted. No friend of Orion's can ever be a lover of mine.

CHAPTER 3
Travel Buddy
DELILAH O'SHAY

S eat belt buckled, I sit on a soft leather seat inside a private airplane. I've booked Orion's charter flights for him but this is the first I've ever partaken. It's quite nice actually. Oh, and I've changed my mind.

Mr. Eleventh Floor's real name is Lynx Grove, he's Treasure Grove's brother and he owns the baseball team! What a coincidence! Apparently, he stays in an apartment on the eleventh floor during baseball season because it's close to his office, which isn't far from the LTI building. He's also attending the wedding, but he'll arrive tomorrow, a few hours before the ceremony starts. Even though he won't be in Vegas until tomorrow, my outlook on the possibility of getting to know Lynx Grove better in the future has improved. I get the impression that he actually isn't a true friend of Orion's. They've only been brought together by way of family ties.

Before Lynx walked away, he said, "Goodbye, Lila," and that he will see me tomorrow. His gaze lingered on my face long enough to make my pulse race.

However, the fact that he knows me as Lila has been burning me up ever since Orion and I got into his car. We didn't have an opportunity to talk about it. He was on his cell phone from the moment his butt hit the driver's seat. Instead of listening to his conversations about nothing important, I inserted my earbuds, closed my eyes, rested my head on the headrest, and listened to white noise in the form of a thunderstorm. The car ride was so smooth and I had successfully put Orion in the back of my mind, so much so that I jump startled when he nudged me in the arm to tell me that we arrived at the airport.

Oh my God, I have never experienced such a smooth transition from car to sitting where I am now. I'm also thankful that the two flight attendants are female and pretty. They should be able to keep my flirtatious boss far away from me for the next five hours. Plus, the aircraft is humongous. It's nearly the size of a regular commercial airplane.

One of the flight attendants mentioned a bedroom and shower at the rear of the cabin. It would've been nice to relax in bed, but I did the math in my head—Orion plus a bed plus a private airplane, no way. Not that he would ever hop into bed with me, I'm not his type, but if this fine piece of machinery is used by Orion on a regular basis, then I can only imagine the semen-stained mattress. I mean, the guy really can't keep it in his pants.

I have no idea where Orion is at the moment. Before leaving me in the capable hands of the flight attendants, he said he needed to check on a few last-minute details. At the moment I'm drinking a hot coffee. I've ordered lobster eggs Benedict with hash browns and fresh fruit for breakfast, which will be served once we've reached cruising altitude. The scent of the food being prepared sits divinely in the air. My stomach growls. I'm going to eat like there's no tomorrow. I don't care if Orion gets a front row seat. I'm sure a woman eating as if she's an actual human being who can get very hungry will be a novelty to him.

My cell phone, which is on top of the wide armrest that offers plenty of space between my seat and the one beside me, vibrates. It's a text message. I look down and see it's from Xena.

Did you serve him notice yet?

I groan, feeling the weight of still needing to complete the task and then type: *Not yet.*

My cell phone immediately dings.

What are you waiting for?

"Cell phone in airplane mode," Orion says as he glides casually past my seat.

I quickly flip over the screen of my device, pressing it against my lap. It feels as though in slow motion I watch him press a button and the backs of the seats that are in front of me flip and now their front sides are facing me.

Orion sits directly across from me. *What?* I stretch my neck and search from the front of the cabin to the back, which is my passive way of showing him that there's so much room, why in the world would he choose to sit there?

My cell phone rings and I know who's calling. It's so like Xena to call because I hadn't responded to her text fast enough.

I quickly answer, turning away from Orion's quizzical glare. "Hi."

"What do you mean by not yet?" Xena snaps.

"So, I'm on my way to Las Vegas," I say overenthusiastically. A forced smile helps me affect the tone much better. "I'm working this weekend."

"For him?" Xena shouts in my ear.

She hates him and it's my fault really—too much complaining to her about how awful it is to work for him. And now in her eyes he's the devil that wears Armani.

"Well, yes," I say, combining my professional voice with my fake smile. "How about I call you after I land and get settled."

"Are you going to the wedding?" she says as if it's the worst thing in the world.

"Yes. Talk to you later. Love you." I end the call before she could ask another question and then promptly turn off my cell phone.

I stare a hole through my lap. I can still feel Orion's eyes upon me. Sometimes he can be so nosy. Unfortunately, I can't avoid eye contact forever. I lift my face and let my eyes meet his.

"I thought you didn't have a boyfriend, Lila."

There's no moment better than the present to address this Lila bullshit.

"Nobody calls me Lila but you, Orion. And I would like it if you'd stop." There…that should do the trick. My voice remained pleasant yet assertive.

Orion frowns incredulously. "Isn't Lila short for Delilah?"

Wrong response, buddy. "And it's not as though you don't know better because I think you do. You had referred to me as Lilly this morning. You know... when you were trying to butter me up for some mysterious reason." *A reason that I think isn't actually so mysterious. He read the letter. He said he hadn't. But I can write the book on Orion Lord and all his behavior points to him knowing that I'm on the verge of quitting.*

Remaining as cool as a cucumber, Orion strokes one side of his perfectly symmetrical face. "Then you prefer Lilly?"

I set my jaw. "Yes."

"But why not Lila? Delilah—Lila, not Lilly."

Just look at him... He looks proud of himself, entitled actually. *Two weeks, Lilly, and then poof—he'll be out of your life forever.*

Resigned to the fact that soon we will be strangers, I say with a slight snarl, "Do whatever you like."

Orion waves a finger. "No...don't leave it at whatever, make the case."

Make the case? My mouth will not close. He and I leer at each other until the captain announces that the airplane is taxiing to the runway. Meanwhile the flight attendants come out of their private room and ask if we would like mimosas before takeoff.

"We're fine, Pippa," Orion answers, not taking his eyes off me.

"I'll take one," I say. I still haven't stopped picturing myself kicking that smug look off his face.

Pippa sets one of two flute glasses on her silver tray in front of me and then sashays to the room at the rear of the cabin.

Now that we're all alone, he asks, "What do you want to say, Delilah?"

With eyebrows pinched together, he's staring at my mouth. I take the tension out of my lips to keep them from twitching.

"Just say it," he urges.

"I'm trying to figure out how to say it."

"Say what?"

"Explain how you just gaslit me. How you're always gaslighting me."

Orion leans away from me, seeming genuinely confused. "I always gaslight you?"

"Yes, gaslight. For instance, my initial request was that you call me Lilly instead of Lila and..." I'm gesturing wildly with my hands.

He coolly raises a finger in objection. "To my

defense, you never offered me the chance to call you Lilly. And I'm not forcing you to question your own judgment. I'm merely asking you a question."

"Hmm…" Narrowing one eye, my mind races back to the start of our chat. He might be right. Shit, I hate it when on rare occasions he's unequivocally right. "Delilah will do."

"Ah…" Orion presses one hand over his heart as if my words have just stabbed him there. "That hurts."

"Flight attendants, please prepare for takeoff," the captain says.

I continue blinking at Orion as I drink my mimosa. It's really delicious. The smooth takeoff and stress-free cross-country traveling makes me truly realize that I'm being abnormally hard on him. Maybe I should dial it back a few notches.

"Then call me Lilly," I say in a rush.

He's smirking victoriously. "So, Lilly, how well do you know Lynx?"

My eyebrows rise and hold. I hadn't expected him to ask me that. "Not well." I sound disappointed about it because I am.

After a moment of thick silence he says, "It didn't appear that way."

I shrug nonchalantly. He's probably right.

There's a high level of sexual magnetism between Lynx and me. I would definitely like to know more about Lynx Grove and maybe Orion's just the man to feed me the details.

"What's his story anyway?" I ask.

He grimaces as if the question I asked him tastes sour. "What's his story? What do you mean?"

Suddenly the airplane is speeding down the runway. My back is forced against the seat as I grip both armrests.

"Is he married? Girlfriend?" I ask in rapid succession.

Orion's expression shuffles through several iterations of more frowning. "Why don't you ask him?"

Even though he's being gruff, he's asked a valid question. "I don't know. We keep our convos pretty surface. I mean, up until today, I've been calling him Mr. Eleventh Floor."

Orion blurts a laugh as the airplane rises to cruising speed. "That sounds like what you name a porn star."

I laugh softly. "I guess it does. Not that I watch porn," I clarify. But maybe on some deep psychological level I've associated Lynx Grove with sex— i.e., banging my brains out. It's been so long since I've done it, at least two years.

"But I don't know much about the guy other than he owns…"

"The Connecticut Ramblers. I know." Woe, this conversation is tilting into girlfriend-talk territory and Orion is not any sort of friend of mine.

"But he's not your type, Lilly. I would steer clear of him if I were you."

I watch him, befuddled about what to say next. I think of the handful of encounters that occurred between Lynx and me. Of course, he's all gorgeous and I now know that he's from one of the wealthiest families in the world. Their wealth wasn't just handed down to them like the Lords. The Groves are nerdy, beautiful, and smart people. Is that why Orion believes Lynx is not my type? Is he insulting me?

"Why would you say that?" I retort.

"Say what?"

"That he's not my type."

Orion interlaces his large fingers with well-manicured fingernails and steeples them in front of me. Maybe the look on my face warns him to tread lightly. Only I don't want him to be careful. I want him to be honest about why he doesn't think I'm good enough for Lynx Grove.

I'm still waiting to hear it, when another long

and lean flight attendant, who's not Pippa, interrupts us to serve us more coffee, sunrise mimosas, and hot homemade biscuits with a selection of dipping sauces, which include peach, apricot, and blueberry compotes, along with chocolate, white chocolate, and butterscotch dipping sauces.

I dive right in and almost forget that Orion still owes me an answer. I've never tasted biscuits this delicious in my life. They have a crunchy and flaky outside with a warm, soft, and tasty inside.

"Umm," I say, all of a sudden feeling happy. Maybe I've been hangry all morning. I was in such a rush to get to the office that I didn't eat breakfast. Missing meals isn't an option for me. But why the puzzled look on Orion's face? He's watching as if he's never seen me eat before.

I flop a hand dismissively. "You know what, no need to answer. It doesn't matter what you think."

"Lynx is not a go-getter, which is why you never knew his name."

I shrug, unaffected by his rather harsh criticism of a man who owns a professional sports team. "Why should I stay clear of a person like that?" There's one more biscuit left. I've eaten three and Orion has had none.

"Go ahead. It's yours," he says, nodding at the biscuit.

Oh my God—who is this person I've become this morning? I never eat without taking the other person into consideration. I've been snappy too.

"I'm sorry," I say. "I haven't been myself today."

He strokes the immaculately trimmed hairs on his chin. Orion never looks a mess. He takes very good care of himself and it seems like he does it without trying, as if he wakes up that way every morning. Yet again, it's unfair that someone like him would have such unprocessed attractiveness.

"Listen," he starts.

I'm waiting for him to finish whatever he was going to say when Pippa enters to serve the breakfast we ordered. Orion asks her to bring us another serving of biscuits. His waffles look fluffy and fruit fresh. My eggs Benedict takes my breath away at first bite.

"So, Orion," I say rather loudly now that we are alone again. "What's the story between you and Treasure Grove?" Oh my gosh, I've been wanting to ask him that like forever.

He smirks. "There is no story."

My eyebrows flash up and hold. "That's not what I heard."

Orion blurts a laugh. "Heard? I didn't know you were a gossip, Lilly."

"It's not gossip if it's true."

Our eyes are locked in a stare off. I'm perfectly okay with letting the subject of his history with Treasure Grove drop. After another long drink of my mimosa, I'll say that to him.

"What have you heard?" he finally says while pouring maple syrup over his waffles.

The mimosas have made my tongue loose, which is why I relay everything I heard about his past with Treasure Grove, including the fact that *Top Rag Mag*, who used to be the premier gossip blog, caught him grinding her ass in her restaurant.

"Also, the way you had me track down your brother and her last spring and summer, that was pretty mad-king of you." My head feels light. I think the amount of alcohol in the mimosas is hiding behind the delicious flavor.

Orion nods coolly. I'm finally able to identify that look on his face. It's a new expression for him. I think the uninhibited posture I'm taking with him surprises him. It surprises me too, but I like this feeling. I'm going to keep going with it.

"Sorry about that, Lilly. That was dickish of me, inappropriate. I'll never give you that sort of assignment again. And the water the other day, sorry about that too?"

I narrow an eye. The water... *What an odd thing to apologize for.* My inner alarm blares like sirens on a fire truck. "Did you see what was on my computer screen this morning?"

I don't take my attention off his face. I'm searching for all microscopic changes in his expression. But there are none.

"No, Lilly." His voice is cool, calm, and collected.

He keeps calling me Lilly. Orion Lord is purposely on his best behavior.

"I don't believe you," I retort.

Orion composedly takes a sip of coffee. "What is it that you're afraid I've seen? Are you hiding something from me?"

Now I see it. I see why he appears as if he's flirting whenever he looks at me or anyone else. "Your eyebrows are thick and low, close to your eyes." *Did I say that out loud?*

"Lilly..." He leans forward, leering at me like it's nobody's business. "Have you had two mimosas too many?"

Yes. "No!" That was too loud and defensive. I pull my shoulders back, showing that I'm in control of myself. "I mean, no."

Orion snorts a chuckle. "I'm not complaining. I want you to enjoy yourself this weekend. And..." He's stroking his chin thoughtfully again. "And to answer your question, yes, I had something with Treasure Grove. It was a long time ago. And yes, I didn't want her and my brother together."

Wow, he told the truth. The next question drops quickly into my head. "And now?"

"Now what?"

"When the officiant asks if anyone objects to this union speak now or forever hold your peace—will you forever hold your peace? Or will you speak now?"

He stares at me, and continues, and continues staring. I wait and wait for him to say something and watch to see if his expression will reveal the answer to my question.

Orion presses a call button.

"Yes, Mr. Lord," a sultry female voice croons through the speaker.

"Pippa?"

"Yes."

"More mimosas. Keep them coming."

CHAPTER 4

Too Close, Too Comfortable
DELILAH O'SHAY

I'm trapped in an odd but brief moment. I hear loud rumbling in my head. Oh no…I've been snoring, and snoring loudly. I slowly start to remember what happened before I fell asleep. I drank more mimosas and ate a few more biscuits, stretching my stomach to its limit. I usually don't have such a robust appetite but there's something about what's happening in my life at this very moment that's making me hungrier and thirstier than usual. However, while I ate and drank, Orion asked me a gang of questions.

"Where are you from, Lilly?"

I said, "I told you many times, even during our interview." Even though Hercules was my first interview for the job and had already hired me, Orion had to approve me. He didn't ask many questions, but where I'm from was one of the few he asked.

"But that was four and half years ago," he said.

"But what about the other many times I told you where I'm from—you're failing to address that part of my answer."

He stroked his chin again. He does that a lot. He's a chin stroker. "Touché, Lilly."

A thrill of excitement raced through me. I had won the argument. I had never so easily won an argument against him. It felt...I can't remember how it felt, but it wasn't bad.

Then he asked my age. It would've been too exhausting to go back and forth with him about a question my boss, who works across from me every day, should already know. Plus, I've also told him my age on several occasions. Goodness, does he ever listen to me?

I said I was twenty-nine. He said I was young. I told him that was a matter of perspective. "Plus, you're not that much older."

He narrowed an eye as if he was challenging me. "How old am I?"

Only he would think what he asked was akin to a trick question on the SATs. "You turned thirty-three on May 11."

His eyebrows shot up as he nodded, impressed. "What do you do on weekends?"

I think it was the mimosas because I didn't second-guess my answer. "I run your errands. I field your calls. I finish your reports. I make sure we don't end up in the basement, which is where you will land on your next fall from glory."

Ignoring my answer, he rapid-fired, "Why don't you have a boyfriend, Lilly?"

His question took me by surprise, which often makes my tongue feel thick, but at that moment, my tongue and entire body felt looser than ever. "Is a boyfriend a need?"

Orion pulled down the corners of his mouth while nodding as if he was pondering an answer to my question. Instead of answering me, he asked if I liked to travel.

I remember wanting to ask, "When do you ever give me time to do that?" But instead, I said, "What is this? A test?"

Orion said he was trying to get to know me better so that he could be a better boss. That's when I found my old friend, Miss Tongue-tied. I knew right then and there that he had indeed read my letter. Before I could really make him confess that truth, Pippa entered the cabin, and stopping so

49

close to his shoulder that her body made contact, she asked if she should prepare the bed for him. She gazed at him suggestively. In his eyes I could see him pondering her request. For some reason I felt slighted. And then I felt uncomfortable about feeling slighted. I shouldn't have cared. I didn't want to care.

"Not today," Orion had said in his charming voice used for mercifully letting down his lovers.

But the flight attendant wouldn't go away. She mentioned how she'll be in town until he flies back to New York on Sunday evening. She said there will be a party tonight and named people who will be there. He mentioned tonight's wedding festivities but said he might stop by afterward. Then she eased him into another topic, which made me close my eyes and turn to face the window. Their voices faded into the distance. I'm certain I heard Orion call my name, but I didn't want to respond as I succumbed to way too many mimosas and a full belly and drifted off to sleep.

However, Orion has called my name again. The airplane is still and quiet. We've landed. I blink open my heavy eyelids, realizing that my seat is reclined and a cozy blanket has been spread over me.

"Welcome back to life," Orion says, flashing his toothy smile.

I DON'T THINK WE'VE EVER TOUCHED BODIES LIKE this. With his arm around me, he's holding me close. There's no chance that I will fall. I am so embarrassed that Orion has to help me down the ramp. Thank God a car is waiting nearby to whisk us away. I don't like being this close to him. His arms and body are too strong and he smells too good.

"Gosh, there's so much sunlight in Las Vegas," I say, squinting at the cluster of hotels and casinos rising in the distance. Then I look up. The sun is practically overhead, so it must be around noon.

"Or you're seeing the effects of six mimosas," Orion says with a hearty laugh.

We reach the last step and I turn to glance at him. Our gazes connect. My lips twitch. I think they want to kiss him.

Get away from him, Lilly.

I try to step away from him, but my legs are too wobbly. Soon enough, Orion is helping me into the back seat. As soon as he closes me in, I rummage through my purse, find my sunglasses, and then put them on.

There... That's better. I let my head float back against the seat and rest it. *What's taking him so long?* I open one eye and turn to see him chewing the fat with Pippa. I groan, unable to look away from them. Orion is never going to change. She's gesturing a lot more than he is. Her face is screwed up as if she's giving him a piece of her mind. I wish I could say I've never witnessed one of his ladies tearing into our office and hurling every derogative name in the book at him. I always bow out of the room to give them privacy. When I return, Orion and I have a funny way of continuing with our day as if the incident never occurred. Finally, I face forward, close my eyes, and wait for whatever's going on between them to end.

Finally, the car door opens and the seat jolts when Orion gets in the car.

"Another one bites the dust," I whisper.

I can feel his eyes upon me. "What do you mean?"

"Isn't she one of your ladies?"

I'm waiting for him to say something, but all that can be heard is the smooth purr of the engine.

Too many seconds of silence go by so I lift my sluggish eyelids as I face him. He's grinning at me.

"What?" I ask.

"Why do you care?"

Oh... I'm tongue-tied again. *Do I care? I don't care.*

I roll my eyes lazily and then close them as I let my body go languid against the seat. "Whatever."

He chuckles, and I'm experiencing a spell of déjà vu. There's something about this moment that feels as if it happened before.

"No, really, come on," he says. "I'm curious. What do you think was happening between Pippa and me?"

I don't give him the satisfaction of opening my eyes and looking at him when I say, "Just forget I ever said anything."

His sigh is almost indiscernible. "I'm a single man. I like to date. I'm looking for the right one."

A cynical laugh escapes me. "Oh, is that what you're doing? Looking for Mrs. Right?"

"Aren't we all?"

I don't have to see his face to know he's leering at me with a charming, come-hither smirk. "Are you planning on charming your way through life while remaining stuck in a rut?" Whoa, finally I said it. I asked him something that has been fixed on the tip of my tongue for several years.

"Then she finds me charming," he replies.

"Like a predator that charms its prey before…" I growl and claw at the air.

Orion lets out a belly laugh.

I shake my head.

"Pippa is an old friend, Lilly. We've known each other for years."

I roll my eyes under my lids. "Then why did she invite you to bed?"

"She didn't invite me to bed."

"Come on. I'm a lot of things but stupid isn't one of them."

"You are a lot of things and you're definitely not stupid."

I sigh long and hard. "Ah, he resorts to charm."

"She thought we were lovers," he says.

Finally, my eyes flick open and I look at him. I'm surprised he's not smirking. His expression is easy, breezy.

I stab myself on the chest with my index finger. "She thought I was…? Surely, she didn't think we were together, together. I'm not your type." My claim feels very disingenuous and I hate that I'm admitting that to myself.

Our gazes remain locked, but probably for the first time ever, I'm wondering what he's thinking. We both know I'm right. I don't wear makeup or flashy and tight clothes, at least not on a daily basis. I have gotten all fancy for certain occasions, but Orion has never seen me that way. And as far as brains go, I'll admit that he doesn't date bimbos. Most of the women he beds are smart and successful but have bad judgment when it comes to men. Basically, he's not the kind of guy a girl gets involved with if she's looking for Mr. Happily Ever After or even Mr. Happy For Now. He's the impossible guy that won't take a girl's call even if he isn't doing anything important at the moment. He'll break a date just to go golfing with his arrogant cousin Nero. And he'll also break a date with a woman just so he can make a date with a better option. The worst part about his worst parts is that he'll hurt a girl while making her feel special. It's a gift he has. I think he learned it by being too close to his mom, Marigold. He's like her golden boy who can't do anything wrong. She also requires Hercules and Achilles to pick up his slack. So, he's spoiled by his brothers too.

Finally, Orion clears his throat and checks his watch. "We have the buffet at six. That'll give your stomach time to digest the biscuits you wolfed down." His magnetic smile is back but only briefly as our car progresses down the busy and famous Vegas Strip. "But by all means, eat and drink as much as you like when you get to your room. The bill is on the bride and groom." He winks.

I tilt my head to study him. Look at him, playing it safe and knowing when to back off. Usually, he would've taken our conversation a lot further, pushing me to an uncomfortable limit, aware that I will not outright lambaste him because he is the boss. However, all morning, Orion Lord has been very tolerable. It's odd. "Tell me the truth, Orion," I say, one eye narrowed. "Did you read the document that was on my computer screen?"

He tilts his head to match mine. "Why do you keep asking me that?"

I'm searching hard for the truth in that expression of his, but I can't find any signs of deception. Maybe he hadn't read the letter. Maybe he's being sincere with all his new interest in me as a person coupled with subtle apologies for being a terrible boss.

The truth is on the tip of my tongue as the car turns up a driveway that leads to the front of a magnificent, over-the-top Vegas-style hotel. But for some reason, I can't speak it. Maybe it's best to stick to the plan and tell him that I quit on Monday—yep, that's best.

"No reason," I say. "Forget about it."

He nods sharply. "I like the sound of that."

My smile falters. That was too easy.

———

It's such a fabulous feeling to not have to check in at the front desk. Orion gives the valet his name and the concierge escorts us to the elevators reserved for VIP wedding guests, which takes us to the thirty-fifth floor. Apparently, that's where the families of the bride and groom are staying. I'm still reeling from the fact that I'm sleeping on the same floor as Xander and Heartly Grove. That just blows my mind. As we walk down an ornately designed hallway, I ask Orion if I am going to meet Xander and Heartly at dinner tonight.

Orion's frown intensifies as he scratches behind his ear. "I hope not."

My eyebrows shoot up. Other than soft Italian opera music and our footsteps the hallway is quiet. Ever since we got out of the car, Orion's been in a foul mood. I suspect it has something to do with why we're here. The wedding is less than twenty-four hours away. His brother will marry a woman he once loved. I think he loved her. I'm not sure Orion is truly capable of loving any woman. Treasure Grove is stunningly beautiful. Maybe he once lusted after her instead of loved her.

"Isn't this a waste of money?" Orion grumbles as we stop in front of my suite. "You know how many poor people they could feed for how much they're paying for this fucking wedding."

"Maybe you should've eaten more biscuits because someone sounds hangry." I smile wryly to let him know I was joking, and sort of not joking.

I'm too tired. I've also had enough of Orion for one day. All I want is to escape into my suite, strip out of my clothes, and enjoy four hours of solitude.

"Yeah," he barely says, frowning at his watch. I keep forgetting how much he loves looking at that thing. You would think he would use his watch to be on time. "I'll knock at five forty-five," he says rather dryly. I actually feel better about leaving him alone when he smirks at me, turning on the old Orion Lord charm. "And if you need more biscuits, I'm sure I can arrange more for you."

On that note I roll my eyes and unlock my door with my keycard. "Ha ha ha."

Orion laughs heartily as I open the door, and then wait for him to move along.

"What?" I say, expecting him to walk away already.

He stretches his neck to peer into my suite. "I'm just checking things out. Making sure everything's okay."

"I'm certain everything is okay. I mean, Xander and Heartly Rose Grove are on the same floor."

"And?" He snarls like he hates the world right now.

"And I'm sure this is the safest floor in the building. What's your problem, Orion? I thought you said—"

"You're right," he says, cutting me off. "See you in four hours."

For a moment, I watch him as he walks away. I can't see his front, but it looks as if he's unbuttoning his crisp white shirt that managed to keep its freshly laundered scent after a five-hour airplane ride. I really hate the way we just left things between us. I shouldn't have laid it on so thick. Deep down I knew that mentioning Treasure Grove's uncle and aunt was just me rubbing in the fact that his brother gets to marry her and he doesn't.

I make a mental note to apologize to him as I

step into my grand suite and then close the door behind me. My jaw suddenly hits the floor as I swoon over the pure opulence of my room. I have never been able to afford to spend a day, much less a weekend, in a hotel suite that looks like this one. Not until this very moment do I realize that I'm actually attending one of the most exclusive weddings of the year. And I've been given unprecedented access because I'm with the lecherous brother of the groom. My face lights up as I let it sink in that I'm in for a fun weekend full of hobnobbing with the Groves, hot famous men, which includes possibly moving things along with Lynx Grove.

My smile grows broader as I toy with the possibility that I too might be able to land a Grove. So, yeah, I should thank Orion for making that possible as well.

CHAPTER 5

Poisonous Apples and Mouse Traps

DELILAH O'SHAY

S till entranced by the opulence of my suite, I
slowly walk through a short corridor, gazing
up in wonder at the hand-painted scenes of
half-naked Madonnas and babies on the arched
ceiling.

Arriving at the end of the hallway, I stop to
regain my breath as I admire the gorgeous golden
silk-upholstered furniture and luxurious jacquard
curtains opened against tall windows make the suite
feel like it's worth a million bucks. Once again, I feel
lucky and grateful to have been invited. But then,
I've earned every penny of my five-star hotel stay
by putting up with Orion's crap for far too long.

The supple mosaic-patterned carpet compels
me to take off my shoes before happily proceeding.

Feet bare, I pad past a gorgeous long dining room table and a black granite-topped island that has a fully stocked wet bar behind it. I step down into the airy living room space. The ceilings are so high, windows so tall, I feel like a miniature-sized action figure. Arms folded, I stand before one of the colossal windows to drink in the breathtaking views of the Las Vegas Strip and a mountainous horizon. All of it makes me feel like I'm light-years away from my issues with Orion. I kind of like him right now. We've never talked as much as we had during our flight. It's as if he's finally trying to get to know me on more than a surface level.

"Hmm…" I sigh as I turn to figure out what to do about all these good feelings I'm having toward a man who has historically irked the hell out of me. But then I gasp excitedly when I spot a remote control labeled Blackout Shades.

I FALL BACK AGAINST THE FIRM MATTRESS. "THIS room is sick, Xena. Look…" I use the remote to engage the blackout shades that are not only in the living room but in my private master bedroom too.

Five minutes ago, before calling my cousin, I

answered the doorbell to my room—*an actual doorbell to my hotel room.* A bellhop dropped off my suitcase and a note from Orion. I attempted to tip him, but he advised me that guests of the wedding are not to come out of pocket for anything, including tips.

I read Orion's message: *Something came up. Meet me at the restaurant.*

My snort was full of accusation, knowing undoubtedly that the "something" that came up has two breasts and a vagina. I'm surprised he asked me to be his "companion" for the weekend. He's never short of options when it comes to women. I still haven't figured out why they keep coming back for more of his crappy treatment. It can't only be his looks. Good-looking men are a dime a dozen. Plus, my species isn't as shallow as his species. So, no, it can't be just his looks. Oh right, it's the money.

"Look at what, Lilly?" Xena says brusquely.

"Blackout shades!"

"I can't see your blackout shades from here, Lilly. Gosh, I really need you to stay focused. I mean, it sounds like you're devouring the poisonous apple."

"The poisonous apple?"

"The apple, Lilly," she shouts. "Don't forget how he thinks. He's trying to woo you. He wants to keep you enslaved and doing his shitty job. Because if you're not doing his work, then it won't get done. And aren't we tired of doing his work, Lilly, aren't we?"

Okay…that was four Lilly's in a row, which means Xena is about to blow her top. I heave a sigh as the dark panels finish completing their downward journey. *She's right.* "You're right."

"I know I'm right, and please don't forget it."

Ouch. I insert a finger in my ear, the one she just yelled in and flip the Up switch on the remote control, raising the curtains again. "I won't."

"Great…good…never forget it. And I think you're right," she says.

I sit up, frowning confused. "Right about what?"

"What you said before the blackout blinds distracted you, remember?"

I screw my face thoughtfully until… "Oh, yes. I remember."

"He knows. Of course, he knows you're quitting. So be careful. He's a sneaky bastard and a charming one too. Don't let him make you forget. Promise?"

My shoulders curl forward when I sigh. I hate when she makes me promise. Xena knows I'm a woman of my word. If I promise, then I'll put myself under insurmountable pressure to follow through. But in this situation, I'm pretty sure my vow will be an easy one to keep.

"Promise," I say.

FOUR HOURS LATER

Okay, so I had taken another itty-bitty-teensy bite of the poisonous apple. Before readying myself to meet Orion, I luxuriated in a warm bath. The tub in my bathroom is huge, jetted, and it's still calling my name. The bubbles smelled like blueberry pie—umm delicious. I plan to bathe again after dinner. I'll make an excuse to leave early.

Dinner starts at 6:30 p.m. The closer I got to that time, the more flips my stomach turned. I have finally arrived at the restaurant and I'm still nervous. A lot of rich and famous people are expected to be here. I've seen the guest list, Jenn, Achilles's second assistant, showed it to me. She and I have become really good friends. We were bonded by Orion's obsession with her boss and Treasure Grove. She could hardly believe he tasked me with stalking them. Jenn and I both agreed that Orion was crazy and worked together to control the situation the best way we could. However, the guest list is why I chose the outfit I'm wearing.

It takes a moment for me to realize that I've stopped to watch Orion, who's flanked by two gorgeous women in chic dresses. Gosh, he works fast. I drop my head to take another look at my outfit, just to make sure I'm fitting in. My dress is shimmering gold and hangs at midthigh length. It has spaghetti straps and dips low at the back. Bottom line, my dress is sexy and so are my slip-on high-heeled sandals. The band around my toes is made of clear and durable plastic and the heels of my sandals are sparkling gold. My outfit looks expensive but it's not. My head to toe look costs ninety-three dollars, all bought off the Home Shopping Emporium Channel. Thanks to Aunt Jolene, Jo for short, Xena's mom, who's the top-rated hostess at the network. Also, thanks to her, I received a twenty-five percent family discount on my outfit.

Completing my self-examination, I conclude that my outfit is just as stylish as the ones the women who are competing for Orion's attention are wearing. Basically, I'm doing a stellar job of fitting in with the rich and famous. When I look up, Orion is already watching me. For some odd reason, fluttering sensations go off in my chest as we don't break eye contact when he says something to the two women. I should look away from him to rid myself of these odd feelings that are occurring in my body, but I can't. Orion strolls smoothly and confidently in my direction, and he's smirking too. Gosh, he's so arrogant.

I'm frowning, I think. I want to frown, but I'm not sure I'm succeeding at it. I hate that he looks the way he does. *Just look at him...* He's wearing the hell out of straight-leg black trousers that melt over the tight and lean muscles in his thighs and his healthy package. Inadvertently, I've glanced at his package on several occasions. He's always been robust down there, but his cock has never excited me at all. Why is that, Lilly? *Because he's a fuckboy, Lilly. Don't you forget it.*

After that little reminder, his package stops distracting me and I'm able to further admire how well he's wearing a short-sleeved black V-neck shirt that shows off his perfectly cut biceps, triceps, and pectoral muscles. And for a pop of color, he has on a brownish-red leather belt and matching shoes—both look very expensive. I can just see Aunt Jo peddling his outfit to hungry viewers ready to buy whatever she's selling. Right now, Orion is proving what I decided about him a long time ago—he's a human mouse trap. *Eat the cheese and he will crush you, Lilly. You will die a slow painful death.*

He's still smirking when he stops in front of me. "Wow, Delilah, you clean up well," he croons.

I frown. I hate that he still smells good. "Thank you," I mumble as I look away from him. I also hate that he's always more handsome up close than from a distance. *He's a ho.* Finally, I can set my focus on his face again. "I see you're already checking out the local produce."

His gaze follows mine to the two women he was conversing with before I arrived. They're watching us. They want him.

"Jealous, Delilah?"

I blurt a laugh. "No." I'm not jealous. I can't be jealous. "No way."

He grunts thoughtfully. "Those two women are my cousins."

I snort dismissively. "And…"

"And what?"

I cock my head to one side to watch him. I don't want to say it, but we both know a woman being his cousin hadn't stopped him from engaging sexually with her in the past.

"What is that look for?" he asks, encouraging me to remind him of what I know—heck, what the whole world knows about him.

Thankfully our exchange is interrupted by loud claps. After all, I'm not supposed to be engaging in verbal spats with Orion tonight. I was supposed to thank him for asking me to be his whatever for the weekend.

Orion's curious gaze lingers on my face for a few more seconds until his eyes widen a fraction of an inch and land on the reason why everybody is clapping. I whip my attention in the direction where everybody is looking. The bride and groom have shown up, walking hand in hand, and they are indeed a sight to behold.

ABOUT AN HOUR LATER

"This, my love, is a buffet." Treasure Grove spoon-feeds Achilles Lord a heaping serving of white-truffle mashed potatoes.

Orion grunts bitterly as he slouches lower in his

seat. "Now she's pretending to be the common folk?" he says under his breath.

Guests laugh. Amusement swirls through the air as Treasure tells us how Achilles claimed he's never eaten at a casino buffet. He had never visited Las Vegas period until their pre-Christmas vacation. Apparently, they've made that a thing, pre-Christmas vacationing, and Orion snorts disparagingly about that too.

"I said to him that he didn't know what he was missing," Treasure exclaims. Her eyes dance in their sockets as if she's the happiest girl in the world.

Achilles Lord nods while chewing as if he relishes the taste of food that his bride-to-be just fed him. I've known Achilles for a while and I've never seen him so easygoing. He and Treasure are proof that opposites do indeed attract and change each other for the better. However, it's abundantly clear that Orion doesn't see it that way. He's been muttering jabs at the couple ever since she and Achilles arrived for dinner, arm in arm, cameras flashing, and guests clapping.

Lips hinting at a snarl, he whispered, "Who do they think they are? The king and queen of the Vegas Strip?"

He's definitely still aggrieved that Treasure

chose his brother instead of him. I mean, why wouldn't she? There are three Lord brothers. It's a toss-up between which is the better choice when it comes to Hercules and Achilles. I guess it depends on what a girl likes in a man. Both are tall and gorgeous. Hercules is just so pleasant and good-natured. I love it when he visits our dungeon of an office. He never fails to ask about my father. Hercules is seated at the table with us along with Paisley. As we mingled and casually strolled around the high-class buffet to taste dishes and program an order for whatever we choose to be plated and brought to us by servers, Hercules once again asked how my father is doing. Of course, Orion looked confused by the question. I keep forgetting that he never cared to know about my father's accident. He's never concerned about much past a five-foot radius from himself.

"What's wrong with your father?" Orion asked minutes later as we took our seats.

I just shook my head. I would've explained, but I became too distracted by the heavy hitters who were taking seats at the table with us. If I lean forward and stretch my arm really far, I could reach out and touch Heartly Rose Grove and Xander Grove. Oh my God, Heartly, Paisley Grove's mother, who is a famous model turned tech guru is more stunning up close and in real life than she is on any magazine cover. And Xander Grove appears just as graceful and mysterious in person too. I'm at the VIP table, that's for sure. I'm also seated among Leo and Londyn Grove, Treasure's parents. And Max Grove, who has brought a date. I think she's his date. Max Grove seems as graceful as his father, but he's more buttoned-up and I detect that he might also be a miserable kind of guy. It doesn't look as if he and his date are at all romantically linked. I'm trying not to stare, but I think he keeps gazing at another guest who's seated on the opposite side of Orion. Her name is Lake Clark and she's an artist. I've actually known Lake for years. We're pretty okay friends. We're not the closest of friends, but she has invited me to many of her famously fun parties.

There are other people at the table that pique my interest too. For instance, Treasure's grandmother Leslie is seated next to Achilles's grandfather Hugo. I recall how last year, Orion gusted into the office railing about how his grandfather had been carrying on with Treasure's grandmother for years. I didn't see why that was such a bad thing and that comment was stuck on my trembling lips after Orion asked, "Isn't that fucking crazy?" I wasn't certain he really wanted me to answer that question or if he was just blowing off steam. It's hard to tell with him.

However, I'm also sitting at a table with Orion's father, Chris. I heard that he's rarely around the family because he owns several bars on several tropical islands. He has a date too and she's not Marigold, the Lord brothers' mother, who also joins us. Marigold is with a young man who's probably my age. Chris's date's name is Caroline. They make a handsome age-appropriate couple. Orion's cousin Nero is also seated with us. He used to come around the office more, usually on Fridays around the time Orion left for the day. It's been nearly a year since I've seen Nero. I'm thinking that might have something to do with his date. She's pretty and seems to be friends with Paisley Grove. The two of them haven't stopped chatting intimately since taking their seats beside each other. Basically, I've sat at my fair share of wedding tables, but this one is by far the best ever and can probably never be topped.

At the moment, my head feels slightly woozy. Since Orion has been such a Bitter Barry, I've been consuming a lot of tasty blue cocktails called the Great Blue Sea just so I can tolerate him. He's called the entire method of picking buffet dishes and then having servers to bring them to our table showy. He also said the food was flamboyant and that Treasure will never change. Well of course the process is showy and the food flamboyant! Achilles is a billionaire! I'm a hundred percent certain he's still in love with her, which sort of obliterates my belief that he can never love anyone but himself.

I think Orion wants me to say something about the comment he made about Treasure pretending she's the common folk.

"This is by no means a common buffet," I say. I'm not sure but that might have come out just a tiny bit slurred.

Orion narrows his eyes at me and I defiantly raise an eyebrow. But I'm toiling to keep it high.

"How many of those have you had?" he asks, nodding at my half-full glass of the blue drink.

I frown, trying to remember the number. "Two, maybe three."

"Try four."

I jerk my head back. "Four?"

"So, Orion," Nero says extra loudly, stealing our attention.

He's smirking mischievously as he extends an

arm across the top of his date's chair. "What happened to Heather?"

I look down bashfully. It feels odd that he's asking about another woman while I'm sitting next to Orion. For all he knows, Orion and I are newly screwing. Maybe it's just that obvious that Orion and I will never do the do, let alone present as a real and serious couple. So, I look up again just in time to see Orion toss back a swig of whatever he's drinking. I think it's whiskey, but it could be bourbon.

"I don't know. You should ask her," he says.

"Are you suggesting she's the one who blew you off?" Nero continues, poking at him like that. I notice the both of them stealing glances at Marigold. Heather works for his mother, which is why she has more access to him than any other woman he's ever dated. And she is high maintenance. I have no idea how Orion convinced her that he would not be bringing her to the wedding, but I'm sure several lies were told.

"Back off," Orion finally snaps at Nero.

Nero drops his head back to laugh. I think he's gotten the response he was looking for. Orion and Nero always needle each other that way. The fact they're close is shocking.

"So, are the two of you dating?" Paisley asks.

First, I'm shocked she was even listening to the back-and-forth between Nero and Orion, she seemed so engrossed in the conversation she was having with her friend. She's not the only one who's highly interested in my answer. Just about everyone at the table is looking at me, even Orion's mother.

Thankfully, my answer is still easy. I snort sarcastically as I lift the glass of my blue drink to my lips. "No way."

"She's your date," Max Grove blurts. The relief in his voice is apparent.

Now everyone, including myself, is watching him as if surprised he said something. He's been so quiet and seemingly bored.

"Interested, Max?" Treasure asks him. "Because I think Lilly's single, aren't you?"

"Hey," Orion blurts. "Leave my assistant alone."

Max Grove's face has turned a gorgeous color of dusty rose. Saying that he's a good-looking man is an understatement, but he's so not my type. I mean, the guy seems like the Grim Reaper of a good time.

"Two brothers down. You're the last man standing, O," Nero says and then kisses his date's bare shoulder. "I'm closer to the finish line than you are."

Orion rubs his scalp as he twists his torso from left to right so that he can scan the room. I'm familiar with that look on his face. His eyebrows are pinched and the corners of his mouth are pulled down into a pout, as he whips his head from right to left, searching the large room. I wonder who or what he's looking for when Caroline asks Treasure if she had anything to do with the food. Her question changes the subject. For all intents and purposes Orion can relax, but he doesn't.

"Let's go," he says as he picks up my plate and his.

He's on his feet before I'm able to inquire about where he's taking me. His family is watching him curiously.

"Where are you going?" Achilles asks, appearing irritated by his brother's sudden move.

"I found us a better fit," Orion mumbles.

TWO HOURS LATER

I've downed more drinks. I stopped counting at… Heck, I don't even know when I stopped counting. I'm at a new table, and yes, the people here are more Orion's speed. The two women he was chitchatting with when I arrived at the restaurant flank him. I'm sitting on the opposite side of the table. There are mostly men sitting with us. I think they're the sort of thirtysomething men who can't let go of their frat boy days. I learned that they're Orion's and Treasure's friends. The two of them used to run in the same circles a long time ago.

All I can say is that switching tables has made me lose my appetite as far as food goes. The two very distant female cousins of Orion's, whose names I can't remember, laugh a lot. They're fraternal twins. I know for certain that they're very distant cousins because they keep mentioning it. I think one of them has her hand on Orion's cock. It's the way her arm angles toward his lap. *Disgusting.*

"So, beautiful," the guy next to me says. His face is too close so I lean away from him.

I frown as if to ask, "What?"

"So, how did the two of you meet?" He flicks

his eyebrows up twice as though he's ready to enjoy an amusing explanation.

My mouth remains caught open. Does he think I'm romantically linked to Orion? Does he think my judgment in men is that bad?

"He's my boss." I sound very offended by his question because I am. I follow the guy's glance down to my breasts. I very much want to fold my arms over them as he continues imagining me topless.

"Is that so?" the guy croons with his eyes still on my tits.

"Hey, Morgan," Orion shouts, waving his fingers, gesturing for the guy who seems to be leaning in closer and closer to me to stand. "Get up."

Eyes lidded, Morgan looks confused but slowly rises to his feet. He's plastered. And I think I am too. In a quick exchange, Orion sits in Morgan's chair and points for him to take the seat he just abandoned. I've never been so thankful to be this close to my boss. That guy Morgan was drunk and starting to become creepy.

"Really..." one of the twins asks, the one with the darker hair. "The two of you never fucked?"

Her pointing finger shifts back and forth between Orion and me.

"Never," I say, shaking my head adamantly.

But they're not looking at me for the answer. Their attention is focused on Orion who's grinning as if he's suggesting that I'm lying. I elbow him in the arm. *Ouch.* That hurt. I rub my elbow. He's made of steel or something. But still I say, "Stop insinuating that I'm lying. We've never fucked. Tell them."

"We've never fucked," he says, gazing into my eyes.

He's screwing with them and me. "Why are you so unserious?" I whine. I'm not myself. This I know for sure. I'm blinking. And he's slightly blurry.

"You're drunk," he says, stating the obvious.

"No, I'm not," I quickly retort.

One of the guys at the table snaps his fingers and a cocktail waitress rushes to our table. His arm ropes her around her waist, definitely crossing a line, as he whispers something in her ear.

Warm breath saturates my ear. "Be careful, Lila. The sharks are circling."

I turn. Orion's face is so close to mine we could kiss. *Yuck.*

"You're drunk and they all want to fuck you," he reiterates.

He sounds crazy. "Who wants to fuck me?"

One by one he points his chin at the men who are seated around the table. They are watching me as if they're trying to figure out how to get next to me. Holy crap, how hadn't I noticed. Maybe because they're Orion's friends.

"But don't worry. I'll protect you."

I blurt a laugh. The thought of being protected by such a scoundrel makes me laugh again. *It's just...* I laugh some more. "The man who..."

I can't get the words out, I'm being choked by my laughter. Everybody at the table is watching me with amusement.

"The man who what?" Orion asks.

How do I say it? I can't even say it. As I struggle to get myself together, the cocktail waitress returns with a tray full of shots. One of the glasses has blue liquid.

"That's for you, beautiful," the guy who ordered the shots says. He's leering at me with pure lust.

"Oh my God," I whisper. *It's the dress—it has to be my dress.*

Orion laughs. "You see. You need my protection, don't you?"

81

"Who is that guy?" I ask.

"Ben."

"Who is Ben?"

"Ben is Ben."

When I shake my head, it feels like it's floating above my neck. "No, who is Ben to you?"

Ben nods at the drink after the waitress sets it in front of me. "Bottoms up," he says with the tiny glass against his bottom lip. His hooded gaze seizes me as his tongue draws slow circles against the rim of the glass.

"Ben is an old friend. But I agree with him. Bottoms up." Orion downs whatever alcoholic beverage that's contained in the shot glass.

I shouldn't do it. Something deep inside warns me not to. I'm already three sheets to the wind. The tiny glass full of blue drink is between my thumb and forefinger. Everybody at the table is on their second shot. The waitress serves me number two before I finish number one.

"Go for it," Orion says. "You're safe in my hands."

I turn to the table full of all the VIPs. I quickly make a plan. If I get too drunk, I'll just return to my old seat and ask Paisley or Lake to walk me back to my room. They'll look after me if I ask because that's the kind of girls they are. I down the drink and I'm shocked by how delicious it tastes. I thought it would be stronger liquor, but it's not. I quickly consume the next shot, realizing that it's more juice than alcohol. I should be okay!

CHAPTER 6

That Night When...

DELILAH O'SHAY

T t's like I'm having an out-of-body experience. I see myself as though I'm not myself. I'm laughing. Lina, Mina, Chase, John, Tucker, Craig. I feel like I've known them forever. Ben, who has curly hair cropped close to his scalp had said something about Yancey's dog showing up at his doorstep last week.

"That's because she's in heat and knows where to go," Yancey replied.

That's why we've erupted into a fit of uncontrollable laughter that feels more like a release of unnamed emotions. I don't know Ben personally, but the fact that the waitress who had been serving our drinks all night is now sitting on his lap—legs crossed, arm hooked around the back of his neck, and fake knockers in his face—says a lot about his character. He's a fuckboy.

But on a larger scale, the pre-wedding night dinner has turned into a real party. I can't pinpoint when it happened. The music came on. A DJ started spinning dance music. Led by Treasure, the soon-to-be married couple was the first to blaze the dance floor and then more people joined them. The air is filled with so much laughing, dancing, talking, and drinking. *So much drinking.* I'm trapped in a state of euphoria. I had a plan before I got this inebriated, but I've forgotten what it was. The plan was designed to keep me safe from Orion's allure. Even though my inhibition has been blasted away, a small part of me knows that I should not have my shoulder against his while leaning against him.

"You two are looking more and more like a couple," Mina says, eyeing us accusingly.

"Ha," I scoff. "You really think I'd be with a man who will let his distant cousin rub him off under the table?"

Mina's face is the epitome of cute—round cheeks, square jaw. She reminds me of a bad little Kewpie doll as she snorts a laugh while inhaling on an e-cigarette like a gangster in a Mafia movie.

"That's very possible as far as Orion is concerned." She winces. "Maybe Lina, not me." She cocks her head in the opposite direction, one eye nearly closed, and a plume of smoke flies out of her mouth. "I'll rub you off before I touch his cock."

I thrust my head back in surprise. I would've never guessed she was into women.

"Once," Lina, the twin who has lighter hair says. At this point, and only because of my condition, hair color is the only way I can distinguish one from the other. "He's good in bed, but I wouldn't recommend him for you, babe. You're too delicate. He'll break you."

The thought of her seeing me as delicate makes me laugh uncontrollably loud. I'm not delicate and I'm strong enough to not give a fuck what she thinks of me. However, I do agree with her on one thing. "I know. I know…" I say past heavy lips. My lips and tongue aren't sharp enough to explain the traffic jam of thoughts waiting to get out of my head. I want to tell the twins that Xena and I talk about how dangerous it would be to fall for a man like Orion all the time. "Xena," I say, slurring my cousin's name and laugh harder. "Xena. Lina. And Mina." *Why is that so funny?*

Orion's warm breath spreads against my ear. "All right, come on. Let's get you some air."

I turn my head. My face is too close to the poisonous apple. I could take a bite. But I wonder if I should leave this venue with a man I loathe so much? Do I loathe him? I like Orion right now, more than I ever had.

"Okay," I sigh, my lips parted.

The weird energy tethering us together has me in a trance. I should kiss him. I really want to. His sensual lips have never looked more tantalizing.

I teeter on my feet. Before I'm able to fall back down in my chair, Orion's firm hands grip my waist, steadying me.

"Be a good boy, O," Lina calls.

"Don't forget to bring her back," Ben says.

Now Orion's arm is curled around my waist. His body is so hard against me. Has he always been this hard-bodied?

"You have such a hard body," I say.

He snorts a laugh. "You really are drunk. Let's get you sober."

Our footfalls land on the concrete. Lots of people are out tonight. Our hotel is so empty that it hadn't occurred to me that we are visitors in one of the most popular and crowded cities in the country. Orion is still holding me close with an arm around my waist. My head rests against his solid shoulder. I need him right now. For one thing, he's essential to my ability to put one foot in front of the other. But there's something else too.

"I like you tonight, Orion," I reveal. "Usually, you're such a..." What is he? He's not an asshole.

"Asshole?" he says with a laugh.

"No," I whisper ardently. "Not an asshole. You're not mean. You're just such a manwhore. And you need a lot of attention. You're so unserious. I also think you're spoiled and entitled. And a certifiable fuckboy." I close my eyes and try to remember what I just said. The word *fuckboy* is stuck in my head. Did I just tell Orion he's a fuckboy?

"You're not wrong." Orion's voice sounds like it's five feet behind us.

"Wrong about what?" I whisper, my eyelids fluttering open.

"All right. I see we have to take a more aggressive approach."

We come to a stop and somehow, I'm facing him, clinging to his hard arms. "Gosh, your body is so firm. There's not much better than a man who's all soft skin and muscle." I squeeze my arms around his torso and press myself against him. "Umm…" I moan.

"Shit," he whispers and then quickly says, "Ellis, pick us up. I'll pin you."

———

I think I fell asleep while hugging Orion, but I don't know. At first, we were standing on the side-walk and now we're in the back seat of a chauf-feured limousine. I'm close to Orion. I like being close to him. The side of my face still rests on his bicep and my fingers skim the ridges of his obliques. I can't stop touching this man that I'm with tonight. I don't even see him as my boss, Orion Lord. He's someone else, a stranger—a hot, remarkably handsome stranger who smells like citrus, pepper, sandalwood, and cherries. I take another deep inhale. "Umm…"

"Let me know if you're going to throw up," he says with a soft laugh.

Orion says I threw up several times on the sidewalk. *I had?* I don't recall. But I snuggle him closer. He's like a big, hard, stuffed animal. "I think I should probably go to bed," I say, even though I don't want my night to end.

"We're just getting started, Lila," Orion says. He draws me closer.

"Are we?"

Was that a kiss he just put on my forehead? "Let me sober you up some. I know the perfect spot."

I can use some sobering up. "Okay," I breathe.

"But we're getting along, aren't we?" he asks.

I squeeze his firm obliques. "Yes."

"You see, we could be friends."

"Maybe," I mutter.

"I read your letter, Lila."

What did he say? Did he call me Lila? "What letter?"

"Returned to the office on Thursday night..."

"Calendar..."

"Power outage..."

"Oh," I say, finally able to decipher his words. "I left because I wanted to have fun."

"Fun?"

I note the intense intrigue in his voice.

"I turned off my phone because I didn't want

you bothering me. Always bothering me..." I mumble.

I ride the movement of Orion's chest as he chuckles. "That's because I trust you with my life, Lila. I wouldn't know what to do without you."

"Poisonous apple," I whisper as I nuzzle closer to him, making myself a bit more comfortable.

"What?"

"You're a poisonous apple and I can't forget it." It felt like I struggled to get those words out.

Orion shifts in his seat. I raise my body, breaking our contact, suddenly remembering that it's best if I keep distance between us. Things are happening within me at the moment. My sex is tingling just a bit. I still like the way he smells too much. And I still love the way he feels too much. But this man that I'm cooped up with in the back seat of a limousine is indeed Orion Lord, king of the scoundrels.

"No, please, come back," he says, curling his fingers, seductively waving me to him.

I shouldn't do it. I should cling to the opposite side of this huge car, but I can't control what I yearn for. "Umm..." I snuggle up against his strong body. "You feel so good."

"So do you, Lila. You're soft."

"Lilly," I remind him.

"But I like Lila. You look like a Lila. Beautiful and exotic. I always wanted to kiss your mouth, you know. Your cherry lips...I always wonder how soft they are."

All of my sensitive parts are throbbing like they have their own heartbeat. Orion has said a mouthful and I've already forgotten half of it. But he mentioned my lips. He wants to know if they're soft. I tilt my head back, pointing my mouth at him and wait for the moment of impact.

Through my lidded gaze I see him staring at me, his lips part, and breaths lather my face. I'm on the verge of devouring the poisonous apple. I'm seconds away from stripping naked and dancing on the mousetrap, and I'm okay with that.

"We've arrived," the driver's voice says through the back seat speakers.

But Orion and I don't move a muscle. I've succumbed to the power he's holding over me. I imagine I'm making the same fatal decisions made by all the women who have come before me. I'm powerless to stop what happens next, only he can put an end to this catastrophic moment of ours.

Suddenly, Orion clears his throat. In slow

motion, I watch his sensual lips go up to my fore-head. He plants a soft, mildly damp kiss on my skin.

"Let me help you out," he says breathlessly.

I'VE SOBERED UP ENOUGH TO WALK WITHOUT leaning on Orion for support. Although his arm is still around my waist, which makes it easier for me to put one foot in front of the other. Our closeness doesn't feel like a big mistake as we enter an elabo-rately decorated Vegas-style lobby. Orion Lord tells the bellman his name and we are immediately escorted to a private elevator. I love that this man is all private elevators and exclusive access. I hate waiting in line, and over time I developed tricks to limit my time spent standing in them. For instance, I have a few favorite nightclubs that I have remem-bered the bouncers' names. Sometimes, I walk by those clubs on days I'm not going inside and wave and say, "Hi, Marquis!" Or, "Hi, Lance!" Or, "Hi, Billy!" Or, "Hi, Don Juan!" People like to be known, especially bouncers.

"Where are you taking me?" I ask as we take a smooth ride up the building. I'm fighting the urge to take advantage of this fine specimen of a man that I'm with. *What's his name again?*

"To another party. But we'll have our own private area and I'll get you a few cups of coffee."

"Oh, Orion."

"What?" he asks.

"I don't want coffee."

I think I just admitted the truth. I prefer the state that I'm in. If I were sober, then I couldn't do this...I squeeze him around his torso and he puts a soft kiss on top of my head.

"We have to get you sober, kid," he says, as if he's the responsible one.

"What about you? Are you sober?"

Orion chuckles as the doors slide open. "Not in the least."

Clinging to each other, we shuffle toward music. My head is light and my feet feel like they're moving on air. I'm loving this night, and this moment. The bass beats drives through me as we make our way down a dimly lit hallway. I barely register that people have stopped their conversations to get a look at us. I can't help but feel proud to be with such a popular and good-looking man.

We enter an amazing nightclub that extends throughout the expanse of the rooftop floor. I gaze up. The ceiling made of glass makes me feel like I'm mingling with a regal sky that's the perfect shade of dark violet. My feet certainly feel as if they're off the ground. The music is still good. I'm being energized by the half-naked and, in some cases, fully naked women and men dancing provocatively on stages that line the perimeter. My shoulders move to the beat. I want to dance too.

Orion doesn't hear me say we should dance. I have no idea where our scantily clad escort is leading us, but I'm suddenly surprised to see the flight attendant from our airplane ride from New York to Las Vegas. I forgot her name although I'm seriously trying to remember it. Is it Pippen, Pepper…

"Oh," I say. "It's Pippa." I don't think anybody hears me. I don't think I can hear me. So, I put my mouth close to Orion's ear as a pinch of something that feels a lot like jealousy charges through me. "Pippa wants to fuck you."

Orion smirks. I can't hear him because of the volume of the music, but I see that he's chuckling. I've never admitted this to myself, but I love his chuckle. Sure, I've convinced myself that I hated the sound of it, but I don't. I never have.

Pippa remains glued to Orion's side until he

says something to her. I couldn't hear what he said but she's stopped in her tracks and we leave her in our dust.

The song changes, and recognizing the tune, my body can't take it anymore—I must dance.

"Dance with me?" I say loudly, tugging Orion in the direction I want him to go.

"You want to dance?" He sounds surprised.

I'm not myself, I know. Or maybe I am myself. I'm behaving like someone I haven't been since my dad's accident.

I answer his question by tilting my head toward where clubgoers shuffle their feet, sway, bounce, and grind to the music. Orion says something to the hostess. She nods and then watches us traipse off to fulfill this burning desire within me. I must curl my body around his. I want to feel him against me.

IT'S BEEN SO LONG SINCE I'VE LET LOOSE LIKE THIS. I sway my hips around Orion, brushing up against him, rubbing his package. He's hard as he mostly stands watching me like a sexy, stalking tree. Yes, I am indeed shamelessly seducing this hunk of a man. I thought I had lost the ability to beguile a man with a sensual dance, but the fire in Orion's eyes, the way he's opened up to me but is paralyzed by desire, says I haven't. My hands are all over his body. I want to show him something. I raise my knee. My talent takes over, allowing me to balance while standing on one leg. I grab my ankle. I activate my abdominal muscles, as I extend my leg high enough to lay my calf against the front of Orion's shoulder.

Heavy-eyed, Orion mouths some words. I can make out only one word—it's *fuck*. I have this man where I want him, which is why I deepen my stretch. The point in my inner and outer thighs ache so good as my pussy is flush against him and my mouth close to his. I bet he didn't know this about me though. "I'm a dancer."

It happens very slowly but now his lips are on mine. I can hardly believe I'm kissing Orion Lord. His tongue, warm and wet, whirls sensually around mine. Our lips tangle. Wow—he's such a good kisser. I am entranced by this activity of making out with him as our lips and tongues continue their sultry dance. I gasp as Orion's large hand grasps my thigh as if he wants me, as if he owns me. Desire makes me moan in his mouth. Who is this man I'm kissing tonight? He's definitely not my lecherous boss. No way… This man is an heir. He's sex on a stick. I want to get to know him better. I want to fall in lust with him.

The song ends and the man that I'm with tonight and I stare into each other's eyes. I'm dizzy.

The moments pass. A new song begins. What do we do next?

"I need a drink," he says, winded.

I let go of a tiny bit of whatever this is I'm feeling for Orion as I nod. I don't need another drink, but I definitely need to sit.

———

THE NIGHTCLUB IS TOO LOUD SO WE'VE BEEN directed to a private upscale bar on the twenty-first floor. No city does sexy atmosphere better than Vegas. The walls are gold-plated and the bar stools are made of glass and glow like light bulbs. There aren't very many people here so it almost feels like Orion and I have the place to ourselves.

He orders himself a whiskey sour and then tells the bartender to make me something blue and fruity, containing the amount of alcohol suitable for a lightweight.

The bartender looks me over when he says that.

Normally, I'd worry about what he's seeing. But all I can think about is how much he looks like a famous actor. I can't remember the guy's name, but he has floppy hair and a killer jawline. Jeez, I can't remember anybody's name.

"That thing you did with your leg…" Orion says now that we're alone.

"What about it?" I purr.

"That was amazing."

I smirk. "I'm a dancer."

"Yeah, you told me that." He says with a hard lift of his eyebrows. "But I thought you have a degree in psychology?"

"I do."

The bartender serves our drinks. His gaze holds mine for a fragment of a second too long. He's flirting right in front of Orion, who doesn't seem to notice. I bet he never notices when a man flirts with his date. I bet he thinks that it's unfathomable that any woman would choose any man over him.

"I see," he says, rubbing his nicely groomed stubble on one side of his face. "Listen, Lila, what can I do to make you stay?"

His question feels like a gentle slap where there's just enough force to sober me a smidgen. I shake my head as I take my first sip of my blue cocktail. It tastes a lot better than the ones I've had all night. And it's not as strong either.

Orion draws his bottom lip into his mouth and wets it. "You like it?"

My tongue is stuck against the back of my top teeth. There's something suggestive in his tone. I'm suddenly reminded how I shamelessly pressed my vagina against him, my throbbing, pleading, and weeping vagina against him. I'm not out of the woods yet though. Holy shit. I want him. At least I'm sober enough to fight the desire to fuck his brains out.

"I do," I barely say. "It has less alcohol." At least it tastes like it.

"That's great. Have as many as you like, then." Orion shifts abruptly in his seat. "But I was saying—"

"I'm surprised you know I majored in psychology," I blurt, not meaning to cut him off. "I didn't think you remembered."

One corner of his mouth twitches, playing with the possibility of forming a wry smile. "I know more about you than you think. But tell me, Lila, what can I do?"

I'm trapped by the magnetic look in his sexy eyes and I am only barely able to eke out, "Lilly."

Finally, his lopsided grin makes an appearance. "I thought you agreed to let me call you Lila."

I shake my head but then stop abruptly. I might have agreed to that. I can barely recall how we got to this particular hotel. One eye tapered, I'm seeing one and a half versions of Orion as I finish off my blue drink and the bartender puts another one in front of me. "You want to know the truth?" I ask.

Orion sits up straighter. "Hit me with it."

I take another swig of my cocktail. The delicious flavor percolates in my mouth. "You're an awful boss." Liquid courage allows me to say that while sitting so close to his face.

His thick eyebrows shoot up. "Okay. I'll give you that."

I shake my finger at him. "You see. You know. That's the thing. You know you're awful and yet you refuse to change."

He throws his hands up as if it's no big deal. "I'll change."

"You can't change, Orion," I say, shaking my head ardently. "And the thing is, you're not stupid. You're a very, very, very...intelligent man. You lack..." The word that was on the tip of my tongue goes poof and I can't remember it.

Both images of him are waiting for me to finish

whatever I was going to say. But suddenly I remember something.

"Did we kiss?" I ask.

Orion tugs my chair close to him and our faces are so close I can feel his breath on my lips. Whatever comprises the aroma coming off him is making my head spin faster.

"We kissed," he admits.

"Oh," I whisper. I remember it now.

"I have ideas, you know."

I think his words are slurring.

I swallow hard. I want to ask him to put some distance between us, but I also want him to come closer, maybe our bodies can melt. "Ideas?" I barely say.

"I know I fucked up, Delilah. We're in the dungeon because of me. But I have ideas."

I'm on the edge of my seat. "What kind of ideas?"

"Something that will put Herc and his fucking software TRANSPOT to shame." Suddenly he tugs my chair closer to his. "I wanted to touch you, Delilah, but I've been exercising restraint. I want to touch your pussy. I want to make you come."

With every blink of my eyes, I'm drawn deeper

into his allure. "You do?" My head is on its way to the ceiling.

"I do."

"You want to know something else?"

I do. I nod.

"I exercise restraint every time I look at you. You're my Lila. When I first saw you, I thought you were the most beautiful woman who never knew she was beautiful. I wanted to unpeel you as if you were a piece of forbidden fruit. I don't want to fuck you hard, Lila. I want to make love to you. Do you slow and steady, make you come over, and over, and over…" His sighs spread across my face. "And over."

"And over?" I repeat. I'm having a hard time following his every word. He wants to unpeel me, make love to me, and make it last.

"Okay," I sigh.

Orion's lips are on mine and then his tongue slips through my awe-parted lips. Slowly, my chest rises towards his.

"Your dancing is sexy, Lila," he breathes.

"Is it?"

Orion slides a finger across my bottom lip. "I want to dance with you again. It gets me hard."

AFTER MAKING OUT IN THE ELEVATOR, I CAN'T remember, but I touched him down there. No...I did more than touch him. I rubbed his hard cock until he seized my wrist and asked me to please stop. And now we're dancing. Orion stands firm, feeling me up, rubbing and gripping my swiveling hips. His finger tracks between my cleavage. He whispers that he wants my tits in his mouth. He wants my pussy in his mouth too. He brings my shimmying body near his firm chest and grinds me with his stiff cock.

"Stay with me," he whispers in my ear.

Our tongues enfold and skim each other. He tastes like home. My heart feels like it's about to burst. "Yes," I breathe.

"I love you," he says.

I think I say it back.

It's as if I'm in a dream, watching him lead me out of the nightclub. My back is against the elevator wall and his hard front presses against my soft front. Orion cups my chin in his hand. His eyes are hooded as we stare at each other.

"I don't want you to ever leave me, Delilah."

I reply, but as soon as the words leave my mouth, I forget them.

He says something else about Vegas being famous for keeping people together. And what he asks me next makes sense.

"Because I hated you, which means I love you," I whisper, I think.

The elevator doors open. And we go. We're going somewhere, and I've already forgotten where we're going.

CHAPTER 7
The Morning After
DELILAH O'SHAY

I struggle to open one heavy eyelid, and then the other. As the seconds tick by I slowly start to come to myself. A sweet and sour taste sits on my tongue—it's a mixture of blueberry and alcohol. Blue drink—I had too many of them. A man's arm, muscular, hairy but not overly hairy, extends across my chest, detaining me against the mattress.

Okay, I think. I'm trying to remember how I got here. But trying to initiate that part of my brain literally makes me feel like I'm slamming my head against a brick wall. I also feel like I'm drowning. I've been hungover only once in my life, after which I promised myself to never get so drunk that I experience the awful condition ever again. But here I am hungover for a second time; and what I'm experiencing now is worse than anything I ever felt.

The man sleeping beside me belts a craggy snore. I turn to get a better look at him. First, I see the back of his head. But I would recognize the back of that head anywhere. It's Orion.

Oh no!

I look down at myself. My heart constricts as my wide eyes shift from my body to his body and then back to mine, and then his. *Wow. He's in great shape.* But shit! I'm naked. He's naked. We're naked.

I want to jump out of my skin and run as far away from the scene as possible.

But there's something on my…

I raise my left hand to my face with the back of it facing me. A ring with a huge diamond is staring right back at me.

"Holy shit," I whisper way too loud.

Orion responds by sawing another log. Shit, he snores loudly. Inch by inch, I slide off the bed. I have to get the hell out of this room. It's not even my room. I wanted to sleep in my piece of heaven last night, not his.

Finally, my right foot touches the floor and then my left. I'm free. Adrenaline pumping like an oil rig,

I bend my neck and touch myself between my legs. *Shit.* I had sex. *We* had sex.

But the ring... I don't know what to do about it. Why would I be wearing a diamond ring? I force myself to look at the stunning piece of jewelry. Maybe it's a gift from Orion or something like that. Maybe we went shopping last night, and even better, I bought it for myself.

I squeeze my eyes tight, trying to jog even the tiniest trace of a memory. I only succeed at making my head hurt more than it already does.

But, yes, that's what happened—I must have bought the ring for myself.

I shake my head. No, that's not what happened and I know it.

Shit.

My eyes dart around Orion's suite. His room puts my room to shame. But I have no time to note the differences. First thing first, I need to get dressed. I scan the floor until my glare lands on my dress strewn across the threshold. His pants are nearby. I guess we didn't waste much time getting undressed. I tiptoe over to retrieve my garment off the marble floor and then try to quickly put it on but the ring gets caught on the hem. But still, I force the dress over my head and hear a rip.

Shit. But I have to get rid of the ring.

I pull the ring off my finger as I pad over to the bathroom. Wow, Orion's bathroom feels like it belongs in a five-star luxury spa. I locate toilet paper and then wrap it around the ring before dropping it into the trash bin.

My heart feels like it's in my throat when I'm back in the bedroom and Orion mutters something as he flips onto his stomach. He's probably going to wake up soon. I have to get out of here. I go on the search to find my shoes and panties. One shoe is on one side of the bed and the other is all the way near the window. I can't find my panties. I know I put them on, but I can't locate them. What the hell happened between Orion and me last night? Our clothes are not logically plopped here or there. I retrieve my shoes as fast as I can and then pinpoint the door. Without a second look back, I scurry to the hallway and get one foot out before I remember the most important thing I could leave behind.

"Shit, my purse," I whisper.

I go back in, tiptoeing around and around until I see my clutch on a large chaise. My small wallet and lipstick are on the cushion beside it. It looks like I haphazardly dropped it on the furniture. What the hell was wrong with me last night? It's not like me to throw my crap around the room—it's not like me at all.

Orion is breathing heavily now, not snoring. I look at him just in time to see his right arm lift and flop down on the part of the bed I abandoned.

Oh no.

I stand very still, praying he doesn't wake up. Several seconds pass and he remains asleep. I take that as a sign to get moving. My nerves are close to eating me up alive as I put one foot in front of the other and keep doing it until I'm back in the hallway and Orion, his suite, and that ring on my finger are safely in my past.

ORION LORD

FOUR HOURS LATER

I wince and suck in cold conditioned air between my teeth as I sit up. My back aches as it smashes against the padded leather headboard. Every muscle in my body is on fire, and my head throbs too. I have a hangover, and on a scale from one to ten it's off the charts.

Ding-dong-ding-dom…

"Shit." There it goes again, the ringing doorbell that woke me up.

"Where the…" *Where am I?* This isn't my bedroom. I try not to let the heaviness in my shoulders weigh me down as I sort out the details of how I got to where I am. I'm in Las Vegas for a wedding. Last night I attended the pre-wedding dinner party. Then I…

Then I…

I rub my palms over my face trying to remember any portion of what had happened last night.

"Delilah," I croak, and then cough to clear the frog out of my throat.

She wore that gold dress like a champ. I wanted to rub my hands all over her body. Her skin looked soft. It felt soft too. My hands remember being on her body. But I can't make out how I touched her or what happened. Last night is not a blur, it's a black hole.

I also remember that Delilah made me hard. It wasn't the first time she's had that effect on me. I'm a man and she's a sexy woman. Hard-ons are like blinking to men. They come and they go and happen without wanting to fuck. But last night, I faintly remember thinking I would burst if I don't feel her around me.

I look down at myself. I'm naked. I grab my cock and hold it.

What the...

It has residue on it. Gunther had entered pussy before I conked out. But whose? Delilah's? I hope not. If I ever make love to her, I want to remember it. And right now, I don't remember shit.

Ding-dong-ding-dom...

I jump to my feet and walk around the bed, searching the floor until I locate my pants. I remember I put them on before leaving for dinner. I sniff them to see if I can smell a woman's perfume. I've never gotten so drunk that I woke alone and with no clothes on. For all I know, my buddies and I went to the gentlemen's club like we planned, and I came home with a stripper.

Shit. "My wallet?"

Ding-dong-ding-dom... "Orion!"

With my hand in the back pocket of my pants, I yank my head back to stand taller. I recognize that voice. *No way is she here, no way.*

"Heather?" I call, stepping one foot into the pants and then the other. I didn't smell her perfume on them, which is a relief.

Before I open the door, I race to the nightstand to see if my watch is where I would normally put it. It's here. That's a relief too.

"Orion, are you in there? Open up!" Heather calls in a sugary voice.

I freeze, experiencing a dose of déjà vu that's tied to my watch. Something happened with my watch last night—something bad.

"Orion!" Heather yells not so sweetly this time.

I sigh hard, frowning in the direction where she's making all of that noise. *What's she doing here anyway?*

CHAPTER 8
Wedding Bells
DELILAH O'SHAY

*W*hat is Heather doing here?

And she's stuck to Orion's side like a magnet. Of course, she looks like a goddess. I, on the other hand, resemble the walking dead, even though I tried my best to brighten my exhausted eyes and take the gray out of my face. Nothing about my skin brightens or makes me look fresh. What was I thinking drinking that much last night? And then to wake up next to Orion too… I have officially lost it.

Before showing up for the wedding ceremony, I paced the small hallway in front of the door to my suite, thoroughly considering packing my suitcase and catching the first flight back to New York. Before then I spent a portion of the morning next to the toilet, throwing up. I even dozed off on the floor in the bathroom. I'd probably still be asleep on the uncomfortable ceramic tile if the maid hadn't woken me up. She almost dialed 911. I had to assure her that I was alive and okay enough to spend the rest of the day nursing a hangover that would continuously make me regret a night I couldn't remember.

It's funny…I used to mock those who said they drank too much and couldn't remember what they did the night before. I never believed that state was truly possible until now.

Regardless, I decided to stay in Las Vegas so that I wouldn't give Orion any cause for alarm. I'm not sure if he remembers being in bed with me. By the way he was snoring this morning, I suspect he also had drunk too much.

Gripped by a pervasive feeling of anxiety, I let my attention roll around the venue yet again. I'm hoping that a face or a voice will help jar my memory. It feels as if we're in a lush garden of a vineyard in Italy. And it's all been set up in one of the hotel's courtyards. It definitely cost a pretty penny to bring this to life. I mean, we are mingling between mazes of real perfectly trimmed bushes which rise hip height. Tall Italian spruce trees surround the perimeter, doing their best to fool us into believing we're not in Las Vegas. There's even a fancy limestone bowl fountain that spews champagne while rich and soothing violin music whirls in the air. The venue is beautiful, majestic, and worth every dime spent to make this a reality.

I identify faces I think I met last night. Yes, Orion and I moved to a different table. We sat with his friends. Two of them were his cousins, twins. *What were their names?* It takes a few seconds before it dawns on me that I'm staring into Orion's eyes. My heart is firing like pistons. He doesn't free me from his penetrating gaze until Heather steps in front of him, commanding his full attention. However, I'm left suspecting that he just might remember what had happened between us. Why else would he look at me that way? That was lust in his eyes.

"Hey you," a man says.

My head hurts when I twist my neck to turn away from Orion to force my complete attention on Lynx Grove. Unlike most of us in attendance, he's fresh, glowing, and unburdened by a hangover. I really don't think holding a party of last night's caliber was such a good idea when your wedding is less than twenty-four hours away.

But still, seeing Lynx Grove always makes me

feel a bit better, and this morning he's having the same effect on me as usual. "Hi, Mr. Eleventh Floor," I say with a pleasant but weak smile, and then hug him.

"Mr. Eleventh Floor?" he asks, displaying quizzical brows.

I laugh softly and even that makes my head hurt. "That's what I've been calling you in my mind. I didn't know your name until yesterday."

I can't help but shamelessly look Lynx Grove over while he laughs. He's wearing tan pants with a matching vest over a crisp white shirt. His five o'clock shadow, curly hair, and the slight dimple on his chin and cheeks gives him male model features. But he's built like one of the athletes on the baseball team he owns. The man is the mere definition of perfection.

"What floor do you live on?" he asks.

He doesn't know. One point lost for me. He hadn't been curious enough about me to find out. "I live on the twenty-eighth floor."

He looks surprised. "The top floor?"

"Yep." We both know that it costs a pretty penny to live that high in our building. "It's an LTI apartment. I'll have to move out when I...quit." My eyes grow wide. I can't believe I revealed that to him. I'm really off my game this morning. I need to get myself together and do it quickly.

He nods as if he's processing what I just said. "I remember you said you work for Orion."

"Yes. I haven't given him notice yet. But I will on Monday."

Lynx smirks and I think my panties melt. "Is that your way of asking me to keep your intentions between us?" Oh my goodness, and he's quick. That makes him even sexier.

"Yes," I sigh with relief.

He winks. "Done."

"Here's my date," Orion says as if we hadn't locked gazes not too long ago. He positions himself between Lynx and me.

I'm struggling to breathe evenly as the tiny hairs stand up on my arm. I cannot be having this acute reaction to Orion Lord. It's as if my body remembers something that my brain cannot.

"Can I get in over here?" Heather says in a tiny childlike voice as she squeezes in between Orion and me.

Oddly, and it seems without giving it much thought, Orion shifts position and moves in between Heather and me.

"How are you doing this morning?" he asks,

head tilted to one side and attention trained solely on me.

My mouth opens. I want to ask him why is he asking me that question. But I have to get a grip. It's not like he asked me to solve a Rubik's Cube. I mean, his question is a rational question, the natural one.

"I'm fine." My voice is too tight. I clear my throat. "And you?"

The twins have joined us, stealing the attention of everybody in our little circle.

"You're Lynx Grove?" one of the twins asks, batting her eyelashes at him. She's shaking his hand before he confirms that he's indeed Lynx Grove.

"I'm Lina and I'm your biggest fan." Her eye contact is so unshakable that I wonder if Lynx feels as uncomfortable as I am watching her flirt with him. "I mean, of your ball team of course."

Oh my God, was that her roundabout way of saying she's a fan of his balls?

The other twin rolls her eyes at her sister's shameless come-on.

"Thank you," Lynx graciously says. Either he didn't get that she was coming on to him or he very much doesn't care. Women must shoot their shot at him all the time. I bet he's a pro in letting them, us, down easy.

"So, where did you two wander off to last night?" The non-flirting twin asks as she slips her e-cigarette between her lips.

Mina. That's her name.

I'm watching Mina, trying to figure out who she's talking to, praying that she's not speaking to me. Suddenly her eyes become giddy. "Oh, fuck, you don't remember leaving together, Orion and Delilah."

"I remember," Orion says. "We got some air."

"Is that all the two of you got?" she says, grinning as she blows smoke out of the side of her mouth.

Right…she smokes like a gangster.

"I heard there was a lot of wine-bibbing last night," Lynx says with a laugh. "Half the people here are hungover, including my parents."

"There was a lot more than wine being bibbed," Mina jokes.

"I'm sorry, are you here alone?" Lina asks Lynx, her high tone disarmingly curious.

She's shamelessly pursuing this man who's a beautiful work of art, and I admire her boldness.

"No. Wait a minute, Lina," Mina says, wagging

her finger. "You two—where did you wake up this morning?"

"In my bed," I say, sounding way too defensive.

"Were you in her bed too, O?" Mina asks.

That's right, Orion's friends call him "O."

"No, I found him in his own bed," Heather exclaims as if she's offended by the question.

Hmm...she must've arrived after I left. I wonder if he had sex with her after he and I did whatever we had done last night. Dear Lord, I want to groan out my misery of not knowing the truth. However, by the confusion on Orion's face, I don't think he knows we were in bed together.

Fingers crossed.

"I was in my own bed," Orion concurs. I can sense his gaze burning a hole in the side of my face, but I refuse to let my eyes meet his.

"Then where did you go?" Mina's like a dog with a bloody bone.

"I don't know. I can't remember," Orion says. "What about you, Delilah? What do you remember?"

"Umm..." I press my lips, trying to recall something, anything—a little something to make it seem as if we had gone our separate ways and hadn't ended up in bed together naked as jaybirds. My breaths are coming quicker as I come to grips with one undeniable fact. I had sex with Orion. Oh my God, we fucked and the evidence points to the fact that we did it without a condom. What if I'm pregnant? What if he gave me an STD? The way he gets around... The women he bangs... Oh God...

"You okay, Lilly?" Lina asks.

My head is spinning. "Huh?" Also, my throat is dry, so I swallow hard to moisten it.

The tip of her finger is aimed at my face. "Because all the blood just drained from your face." Her cheeks blow out as she stifles a laugh.

"Leave her alone, Lina. It's clear they left together, but she was too drunk to remember what happened afterward," Mina says. "She was terribly inebriated. But you weren't so fucked-up, O. Let her off the hook already."

Orion grimaces as he looks off. *Oh my goodness, he can't remember either.*

"I took her out to get some air."

"And then?" Mina asks.

"And then..." Orion cocks his head to one side. "We went to Abracadabra."

"We didn't see you there," Lina says.

"But we arrived at around what, two," Mina reminds her.

Why did I let my gaze connect with his? He's watching me so intently that my head is spinning. I'm on the verge of admitting that I woke up in his bed. I think he already knows.

"That's where I lose track of time," he says, watching me as if he's willing me to recall what happened.

"But you woke up in your own bed?" Lynx asks.

I quickly turn to face him, happy to be released from Orion's spell, and then nod stiffly. "Yes." *No.*

"Then that settles that. You went back to your own room and went to bed." Wow, what a way to "Svengali" our little situation. I would like him even more, but surprisingly, I'm having a hard time doing that when Orion is standing so close to me. What are these emotions swirling through me from head to toe? They're nonsensical. I can't feel this way, *I just can't.*

"It seems so," Orion says with a quick pinch of his nostrils as he eyes Lynx suspiciously.

My face is warm and I hope my skin hasn't turned red. I slowly set my attention on Mina, who's grinning at me as if she's figured out the truth. I'm not sure she has though. I think she's just amused by the possibility.

WE'VE DISPERSED AND HAVE TAKEN OUR SEATS. Orion stands in line with the other groomsmen, grimacing as if he hates it. I watched Achilles talk him into being part of the wedding party. The Lord brothers have a strange dynamic. I've been trying to figure it out ever since I started working for LTI. They never force Orion to fulfill major obligations —only the insignificant ones. I always believed that Orion suffers from having low expectations set for him. Hercules is the golden boy and Achilles is the enforcer. But Orion is the one who always has to be managed while his brothers do the important crap. I actually feel sorry for him standing up there with a front row seat to his brother marrying the only woman he ever loved. *Look at him, standing up there all miserable.* It's the ultimate slap in the face. I should tell him the truth, and even fess up about the ring. We should definitely try to figure out why I was wearing one.

"He's handsome, isn't he?" Heather whispers in my ear.

I jump startled. She's sitting next to me. I rip my gaze off Orion. Shit, I've been staring at him. It's only when I look away from him that I realize he's been staring at me too.

I shrug indifferently. "I don't know," I whisper.

She's smiling like a new convert of a cult. "Well, he is, and we are going to make it official very soon."

I detect a final phrase to what she just revealed, but she's choosing to leave it unspoken. But it goes something like this: so, leave him the fuck alone. Or...so don't ever wake up naked in bed with him again with a diamond ring on your finger because he belongs to me.

Thankfully, the wedding march strikes up. I don't know how to feel about the strange exchange between Heather and me. I've been staring at Orion for so long that I hadn't noticed the groom has already taken his position. So now is not the time to think about Heather. But oh boy, does Achilles Lord steal the show or what? He is the epitome of what a man should look like on his wedding day. When Treasure makes her appearance in an elegant and effortless white silk gown, he is so captivated by her that even I feel as if they are the only two people in the garden. Suddenly, my night with Orion isn't on my mind anymore. I am in the presence of, encapsulated by, and privy to a display of true love.

THE COUPLE HAS JUST FINISHED EXCHANGING THEIR vows that were at times humorous and heartfelt. I was on the edge of my seat when Achilles told Treasure that she was his breath, blood, and best friend. I believed every word he spoke and thought I'll probably never know how it feels to be loved that way.

"Now, Achilles Lord, you may kiss your bride, and you, Treasure Grove, may kiss your groom," the officiant, who is a very serious middle-aged man pronounces. According to Jenn, the officiant was Achilles's choice. Treasure had chosen the venue and all the unconventional wedding activities like last night's party. She even wanted his cousin Nero to preside over the ceremony but Achilles said, "Absolutely not." He had taken the hands-off approach with everything else, but he wanted a serious wedding ceremony, which for him meant a real ordained minister who has a British accent. Treasure said, "Deal," and that's how we ended up in Las Vegas. Now that I think about it, she's the reason for my woes and my hangover.

"May I present to you Mr. and Mrs. Achilles Lord," the officiant proclaims.

Yes. I heard from Jenn that Treasure has zero hang-ups with being referred to as Mrs. Achilles Lord. She likes being reminded that she chose well when she chose him. The newly married husband and wife don't hesitate before they go in for another smooch. I'm having a visceral reaction to their kissing. I catch a flash of Orion's face up close in a low-light setting. I rub my damp palms over my thighs and then clutch them. He was close to me at some point last night, before the obvious sex that we had. *Oh no, what have we done?* I shout on the inside.

Then my petrified gaze lands on Orion and he's watching me too.

AFTER THE CEREMONY, I FELT LIKE A ZOMBIE AS I follow the procession of guests down a long walkway designed to make us feel like we're taking a wedding stroll down a quaint street in Venice, Italy. Orion is walking with the groomsmen and they're all singing a song I've never heard. Now might be the time to duck out and leave for home. Tomorrow is Sunday—Orion and I are supposed to fly out first thing in the morning. Five hours on the airplane with him alone seems like an impossible task to complete. I can't be alone with him until I figure this out. This, meaning the brand-new attraction I have toward him.

"You've turned green," Mina says. She's now keeping step with me. "Still sick from overdoing it?"

I nod, only half lying. My stomach and head still aren't in the most pristine condition, but what's mostly making me feel ill is the fact that I can't remember my night with Orion.

"I feel like shit too."

"What's the song they're singing?" I ask, figuring she may know it.

Mina rolls her big bright eyes. "Some frat boy number."

I laugh a little. The twins are a good time, that's for sure.

We file into a wide-open space decorated with beautifully adorned tables and chairs. It's all so ornate that I feel that we've stepped into a banquet room at the Vatican. I can't help but seek out Orion. Heather has fastened herself to his side, and has so boldly taken the seat that was reserved for her until he broke their date and now it's supposed to belong to me.

"Come sit with us," Lina says. Her arm is already linked around mine and she's guiding me to her table.

HEATHER'S MILKING HER NEARNESS TO THE GROOM'S brother and the last unmarried Lord brother for all it's worth. She's touching Orion on the arm a lot and whispering in his ear. Occasionally his gaze finds mine, especially after he gave the most awkward and quickest wedding toast in history.

"I hope you make it. Good luck," he had said and then sat back down.

Everybody at my table fought back their laughter except me. I didn't want to laugh at all. I feel so sorry for him, and I should not be feeling sorry for him. But after the last time our gazes met and butterflies fluttered in my belly, I decided to pretend he's not here. That strategy has been working so far. The misfits are a fun group. They've rapid-fired dozens of questions at me. They know about my dad's accident and how much LTI pays me. They know that I had to take the job and be

Orion's servant instead of pursuing my own dreams of being a Broadway dancer or a psychologist. I hadn't figured it out yet. However, I promised to show them my best dance moves when the band strikes up.

I've learned more about some of them too. Ben is a Wall Street trader and hates his job. Carl is an associate producer of a nighttime talk show. Chase is an English teacher and an author of two very long sci-fi novels. And Lina is a book editor and Mina is a literary agent. Our conversation has variety. We talk famous people who they've had personal encounters with, some good and some awkward as hell. They chime in on their experiences with the same people. They all agree that the person is cool or an asshole. At the moment, they're making a bet about whether or not Heather will be able to rope Orion into marry her.

"She's clearly working on it," Mina says, still smoking her e-cigarette like a gangster. If I smoked, I would mimic her style, I find it so alluring.

I still try to keep my gaze away from the VIP table where Orion has been chopping it up with his family. The last time I accidentally let my eyes graze over him, he still looked miserable.

"Well, she's doing a fine job keeping him away from this one," Lina says.

All eyes take notice of me.

I slap a hand on my chest. "Keep him away from me? Why would Orion have to be kept away from me?"

"You really need to ask?" Mina winces, exhaling a perfect billow of smoke past her twisted lips.

I really don't know how to respond to what she just said. Other than, "I've worked for Orion for four and half years. He's been…" I feel like running him down is the wrong thing to do in this situation.

Mina peps up as she takes the cigarette out of her mouth. "He's been what?"

"Never interested in me, and vice versa," I say.

She snorts a laugh. "Weddings can do that to you."

I frown. "Do what?"

"Change dynamics."

I shake my head. She's crazy. There will be no dynamic changing between Orion and me. I think the only reason he's been on his best behavior is because he doesn't want me to quit. I do his work for him, and that's all he's concerned about preserving.

Zeroing in on me, Mina's lips part as if she's

going to say something else but the music strikes up. The table bursts out in laughter after Achilles playfully dedicates the first song to his wife, which is "Super Freak" by Rick James. My eyes find Orion's and he's laughing. Even he has to concede that the paradox of his uptight brother getting the band to play that song for Treasure Grove is funny.

"Delilah! Time to show us what you got," Ben says, taking off his vest while rising to his feet. His hand is outstretched toward me. He wants to be my first dance and I'm willing to fulfill his wishes but a body is standing next to me. I look up and into the eyes of one gorgeous man, and he's not Ben.

"Shall we dance?" This other fellow asks.

CHAPTER 9

I'm Not Jealous

Delilah has been avoiding my attention to her throughout dinner. And now she's dancing with Lynx Grove. What's his deal anyway? He and I have hung out in the same circles twice or maybe three times in the past year. There was the bachelor party. A stripper wanted to dry hump him and he wanted nothing to do with her. I had thought he wasn't into women, and frankly, to each his own, but I can now see that I guessed wrong.

"Orion, I think we should talk, go somewhere private," Heather shouts over the music.

I'm set to respectfully decline going anywhere with her. I know what she wants, and I'm not in the mood to give it to her. Delilah is twirling rapidly like a ballerina. I absentmindedly rub my chest as I see a snapshot of her dancing around me. Her leg is up, ankle on my shoulder. I resist the urge to slip my fingers inside under the crotch of her panties and then inside of her. I sense that I wanted to see how she looked when she climaxed. And I saw her face when she let go. My cock tightens as it grows.

Did we....?

"Orion, did you hear me?" Heather shouts in my ear.

"Shit." I'm on my feet. Heather has been like a fucking gnat. The only reason she showed up is because my mother told her I was here and that the card at our table had her name on it. She took that as proof that she was still on the guest list, and hopped on a morning flight from JFK to Las Vegas. She told the people at the front desk that she was my girlfriend and would be sharing a room with me. I've allowed Heather to impose her will on me for the two months I've been doinking her and she's been doinking me. Our sex has been motivated by mutual lust, the fleeting kind, and we both agreed it wouldn't go anywhere. Now she's trying to change the plan. Before the ceremony started, I went down to the front desk and made sure Heather was given her own room far away from mine and made sure her access to our private floor was revoked. I don't want Delilah to get the wrong idea.

Delilah has stopped twirling her sexy body. She's such a good dancer. Her moves are smooth, graceful, and concise. I can stand along the sidelines and watch her dance for hours. I stop in my tracks when Lynx pulls her close as the fast song ends and the slow song starts.

"What the fuck, Lynx," I mutter. He wants to wait until this weekend to make a move on her?

Her arms are around his neck and her eyes are closed as they sway to a catchy tune about a guy being head over heels and it shows.

"Orion," my brother Hercules says loudly as his palm slams down on my shoulder. I absorb the sting as if it's nothing as I force my attention off Delilah to glare at him.

"What do you want?" I ask with controlled agitation.

"Good call bringing Lilly. She and Lynx seem to be getting along. I can see it." He's grinning, watching them proudly, almost like he's the one who's responsible for them dancing together.

"See what?" I snap.

"The two of them together. She's been a serious asset to us. It'll be great to get her in the family so she won't run away from your ass, and we'll never see her again."

I scoff as my hand comes down so hard on his shoulder that he dips low. I bet it hurt. "Always business with you, isn't it?"

"And not enough with you. Listen—" he starts.

"Not now, Herc," I say, before he's able to get started.

"I need you to figure out how to squeeze..."

I'm walking away from him, eyes fixed on Delilah as her chin floats up and she laughs at something Lynx has said. I can't imagine Lynx Grove saying anything that humorous. He's not a witty guy. She's laying it on thick, that's what she's doing. I'm trapped between stomping over there and cutting in, and just walking the hell away from this fucking reception. I've had enough for one day. I can't believe I let Achilles rope me into being a groomsman and making that damn speech. He only did it because he needs to see that I'm really okay with him marrying the one woman I ever thought I loved. I'm okay with them getting married *now*. But fuck, what if I weren't okay with it? It's not as if he'd ever break up with her for me. So, what's the fucking point of needing me to be okay with it? My brothers are mysteries to me. I'm this close to taking a long break from both of them.

Delilah and Lynx are whispering back and forth into each other's ears. Now *that*, the two of *them* together, I'm not okay with that shit. Suddenly Mina appears beside me, arms crossed, and that cocky little smile of hers glowing.

"Cute couple," she says, knowing she's getting under my skin.

What's wrong with my fucking family? Don't they care about me? I have Herc on one side unable to see that I'm steaming mad and on the verge of losing it because Lynx is making a play for my assistant. I have Mina on my other side, my cousin Nero's sister, aware that I'm feeling something for Delilah but making a mockery of the fact that I'm losing to a fucking Grove. Fuck her. Fuck him too. Fuck them all. I'm going to bed. I turn on my heels, leaving them all to their dancing. My strides carry me back to my room faster when it hits me that later tonight, Lynx has a high probability of scoring with Delilah.

"Fuck!" I shout in my head. *Fuck.*

TEN HOURS LATER

I didn't get a lick of sleep. I tossed and turned all night. I almost got out of bed and went to Delilah's room to find out if she was there. But I didn't. I couldn't. I forced myself to get a grip instead. I can't be with Delilah anyway. I need her too much. I don't want to fuck her, and fuck her, and then fuck her some more until *kaboom*. But eventually, I stopped listening to my inner warning system. I'm at her door ringing the doorbell and knocking, but nobody's answering. I want to blow my top because I'm certain that she's in Lynx's bed right now and our flight leaves in less than an hour. It's not like her to be this irresponsible. The old Lila, pre-boning Lynx Grove, would've been at my door a half an hour ago making sure I wouldn't make us late.

I call her cell phone and it goes straight to voice mail. I follow up by calling Lynx. I don't give a damn. He's fucking my assistant. She belongs to me.

"Hey, Orion?" Lynx sounds drowsy and curious.

"Is Lila with you? Our flight leaves in half an hour."

"Oh…she flew back to New York last night," he says.

It's as if I've been hit in the face with fluorescent light. "She did what?"

CHAPTER 10

Let's Make a Deal

DELILAH O'SHAY

MONDAY MORNING

If I had flown all the way back to New York with Orion, I don't think I would've been able to keep the fact that I woke in his bed on Saturday morning to myself. But that's not the real reason why I packed in a huff and took a commercial flight all the way back home. I was looking forward to more biscuits for breakfast sans the mimosas. As it stands, I'm never drinking alcohol again, or at least not for a very long time. This is why I really left Las Vegas. After dancing with Lynx and then Ben, I looked around for Orion, but he was gone, and so was Heather. He went off to have sex with her because that is what he does. He bangs women he's "in a relationship with" several times before he starts breaking dates with them and then asks me to send them a bouquet of flowers with a card that reads: *Thank you for the fun we had. It's time I move on, and I think you should too. But I'll always be here for you if you need anything, just call. Your friend, OL.*

I don't ever want to get those flowers with that card from "OL." I have a feeling I'll be sending a bunch to Heather today. I hate to admit it but that's wishful thinking. Heather is not like all the others. She's also hard to compete with because Orion's mother loves her, and he's a mommy's boy. Unlike Hercules and Achilles, Marigold exhibits nothing but pure admiration toward him. That's why he'll do anything to make her happy, which includes probably making it work with Heather.

Anyway, believing that Orion and Heather skipped off to his more elaborate suite to bang each other's brains out, I called Xena and confessed that I woke up in his bed that morning. I didn't tell her about the ring though. The ring stinks of a major fuck-up on my part. I think if I give my brain a few days to reset and recover, then I'll remember exactly how it came to live on my finger.

Xena yelled warnings and I-told-you-sos until her throat turned hoarse.

"Get away from him, Lilly. Come home now."

I knew she would say that, which is more than likely why I called her.

"I'm leaving now," I had said. And then that's what happened.

Last night before bed I drank a cup of chamomile tea and ate a tuna sandwich. Usually that's the elixir to help me get to sleep and it worked. But as soon as I woke up, I was anxious again. Today is the day I serve Orion notice.

I left for the office early and now here I am sitting at my desk, waiting for him to show up late or maybe not at all. If he so happens to behave like a serious boss and comes in today, then I'll hand in my two weeks' notice, which is already printed, signed, folded neatly, and sitting on his desk.

To distract myself from thinking about the inevitable, I got right to work. So many times I wanted to race across the office and feed my letter through the shredder. But I couldn't do it. No matter how great my weekend was, Orion Lord is still a shitty boss. Inviting me to the wedding was all tactic on his part. Despite my fancy room, his fun

145

friends, his airplane's delicious biscuits, and seeing a side of him I never knew existed, I will not continue working for him.

"Morning," Orion says, gusting into the office like an unforeseen tornado.

"Oh, you're early," I say for lack of better words.

My gaze moves up and down his physique. Orion looks absolutely, undeniably, and heart-stoppingly delicious this morning. The burgundy pants he has on hugs him in all the right places and so does his black polo shirt. And, as usual, he smells like temptation if temptation had a scent.

"Lynx Grove, huh?" He drops down in his large chair; his perfectly tight buttocks makes a loud thud.

For a second, I catch him glancing at the notice I put on his desk. Instead of picking it up and dealing with it, Orion's chair squeaks as he leans back and stacks his hands behind his head. He's waiting for me to respond to his comment about Lynx.

I sigh, recalling how we ended our third back-to-back dance on Saturday night.

"What about him?" I ask.

"The two of you were getting along well."

I shrug indifferently. "He's nice."

"And…"

"And nothing."

He pins me with a curious gaze. Yes, I absolutely want to blurt out that by the end of our final dance, Lynx revealed that he likes me and if his circumstances were different, he would want to get to know me better. But he thinks he's falling in love with someone, an old friend. Then I did something that surprised even me. I kissed him on his gorgeous cheek and told him he was a classy guy and that I liked him too. The song ended, he bowed, escorted me off the dance floor, and then we parted ways. When I saw him next, he and Treasure were dancing together. Everybody watched as Treasure tried her best to lead him in a dance routine they had made up when they were kids. It was fun watching them. They were cute. I'm not going to lie—I envy the lucky girl who ends up marrying into the Grove clan. It would be fantastic if *she* was me, but I'm pretty sure that will never be the case.

My shoulders feel jittery when I shrug again, trying to appear even more indifferent than the first time. "He's in love with somebody else. I guess unlike somebody we both know, he can have sex with only one woman at a time." I would've said *fuck* but we're at the office where I endeavor to keep things professional.

We glare at each other in silence. However, I can't play the whoever speaks first loses game with him, *at least not right now*. I've got too much on my mind.

I fold my arms across my chest. "But you and Heather were making up for lost time?" My accusatory tone doesn't get past my own ears.

Orion's eyebrows ruffle and then even out. "Heather?"

"You disappeared together."

There's my least favorite cocky smirk. "Where do you think we went?"

"I don't know. You tell me."

He taps his finger on top of my notice as he studies me for several seconds. I wonder what he's thinking. He's definitely pondering something that has to do with my inquiry about Heather and him. He must see through me. He knows I'm jealous which is why I smile big enough, attempting to wipe the evidence of how I really feel of my face.

"I didn't spend the night with Heather," he admits, still grinning.

I toss my head into a curious tilt. I actually believe him. "Why not?"

"Because I was tired, Lila."

"Lilly."

He picks up the letter and continues staring at me as he unfolds it. "Lilly, I know what this is and I don't accept it."

I drop my arms and sit up straighter. Okay, it's time—the moment has arrived.

"It's your two weeks' notice." It's as if he's moving in slow motion as I watch him read what I've written on the page. When he makes it to the end, he grunts thoughtfully. "I kind of preferred the rough draft."

My jaw drops as I gasp. "Then you did read it."

Orion nods sharply. "I had."

"You lied to me."

"Sorry, Lila."

"Lilly. And you don't sound sorry at all."

Orion turns his sexy chin slightly and frowns contemplatively. "I thought we had made an agreement that I can call you Lila. It's out of love, not disrespect."

I'm rendered motionless. Did he say love? I feel like he said that to me before, and I said it back to him. The details are fuzzy, but I'm so uncomfortable on the inside that I readjust in my seat again and again.

"We'll get into the matter of Lila versus Lilly later. But first…" He springs out of his chair to sit on the front edge of his desk.

Do not look, Lilly. Do not look at his package, which is begging me to admire it.

"What do you need from me?" Orion asks.

"Huh?" I don't know what's happening to me right now. I'm all discombobulated and not in control of my desires.

"What can I give you to make you stay?"

Oh. I gently shake my head. "Nothing. You can't make me change my mind."

"Sure I can. You're leaving because of me. How about I make you stay because of me?"

He crosses his ankles, making his bulge appear plumper. What is wrong with me? I rub the side of my increasingly warming neck.

"Okay, so you don't like it when I call you after normal business hours. Done. I'll stop."

My chin juts out. "Really?" I'm surprised he's giving up the ability to do that since he does it so often.

"Sure. I won't call you, unless it's personal."

I shake my head like a rattle. "Personal? Why would you need to call me for something personal?"

"I thought we got pretty close this weekend."

Three things happen to me at once. I fight the urge to drop my jaw. I forget to swallow, which allows saliva to slide down the wrong pipe. And now I'm coughing to keep from choking. "What do you mean?" I strain to say.

"You need some water?"

As if he's going to go get me water. *Huh!* I shake my head. "No, I just…"

"Wait." He's on his feet. "I'll be right back."

I cough even harder now that I'm alone, working arduously to clear my throat before he returns. And he's back carrying a bottle of cold water. I did not think he would go into the supply room to get me water. He's never done that before.

"Thank you," I barely say, leaning away from him untrustworthily as he sets the bottle of water in front of me.

"You're welcome." He's regarding me with the kind of smirk that never fails to melt panties.

"But still, Orion." I cough one last time to finish clearing my windpipe. "I'm choosing to do other things with my life."

"Really?" He folds his arms again. "Like what?"

"Dance."

"That's right. You dance. You told me that."

I'm trying to remember when I told him that. "I did?"

He grimaces. "Yeah."

Telling him the truth about where and how I woke up on Saturday morning is on the tip of my tongue. But I can't speak the words.

"Your lips are quivering again. What do you want to say to me?"

I press my lips to stop them from fluttering. I really have to stop doing that, especially since he knows why I do it. It's a weakness and I cannot show weakness around Orion.

"What do you want? Broadway?" he asks.

How did he know? "Yeah," I say tightly.

"Done."

"Why?" I ask, squishing my face as if repelling his offer. "Nothing ever comes for free with you."

Orion jerks his head back as if offended by my claim. "That's not true."

I grunt. "This negotiating that you're doing is evidence of you doing nothing for free. Which actually scares me, Orion. I want you to be more tolerable because you're making real foundational changes, not because you want me to stay and do your work for you." I sigh hard, proud I didn't curse at him.

His hand flies up. "Foundational changes," he muses. "I like that."

I grunt as I roll my eyes. "You're impossible."

"I'm impossible?"

"You're mocking me."

He puts his palms on his chest and leans toward me. "No, I'm not, Lila," he says in the sincerest tone.

"It's Lilly," I practically yell while shaking my fists.

"Okay—Lilly," he acquiesces.

"Thank you."

"Give me a list. What do you need me to change so I can get you to stay with me for two more months?" He's rubbing his palms together.

"Nothing. I'm leaving."

"Come on. Humor me. Just humor me."

I narrow my eyes. Look at that face, every angle is too perfect. I can't believe I've been looking at him for four and a half years and hadn't been the least bit aroused by him. I want to hate Orion, I really do. I thought I did hate him. But look at his face…

"You haven't told me why you want me to stick around for two more months," I say. What he tells me will determine if I even entertain this deal he's trying to strike.

"Oh, that's easy," he says, shrugging his eyebrows twice. "I want to get back to the penthouse floor. You liked the top floor, didn't you? It's all plush and brimming with benefits." He's shaking his finger as if he just remembered something. "You used to rave about the bathrooms up there."

Well...he's got me there. The top floor used to definitely make putting up with his bullshit almost worth it.

I sigh, letting go of some of my fight. "I'm listening."

"I have been working on something," he says.

"Like..."

I sit back in my chair and swivel, feeling proud to be the one who momentarily has the upper hand. But he seems reluctant to tell me what he's been working on. "I thought you said you could trust me?" Then, I jerk my body so hard that I nearly fall out of my seat. "Wait. Is it AI?" I can't believe I just remembered that. I actually see us sitting in a bar that had chairs that glow like light bulbs and him telling me that.

Orion frowns confused. "Yeah...how did you know?"

"I think you told me on Friday night."

Orion nods contemplatively. "Yeah, I must have told you, otherwise how would you know?"

We stare at each other mystified.

"What went on between us on Friday night?" he asks.

My shoulders curl over at the end of a big sigh. "I wish I could remember."

"Do you remember me going off with a woman?" he asks.

I could lie to throw him off my trail. "I don't." That didn't sound too convincing as far as I'm concerned, but I think Orion bought it.

"Right," he whispers and then suddenly springs to his feet. "Well, listen. What will it take to get you to work for me for two months while I finish getting my AI software off the ground?"

Wow. "Your AI software?" Orion associated with such a hefty undertaking feels so improbable.

Orion nods. "I've been working on it for a while."

"A while?"

He waves my two weeks' notice as if it's a white flag. "After two months we'll revisit the matter of this notice."

I shake my head fervently. "There will be no

revisiting of the notice, Orion. I'm quitting. I can't work for you anymore."

"Aha," he says poking his finger at me. "Then you are quitting because of me."

My lips do not stutter when I say, "Of course I am. But you're not the sole reason."

Orion claps his hands. "Okay, Delilah, let's cut the bullshit back-and-forth. I need you. So, what do I have to do to keep you for two months, at least?"

The two months crap unsettles me, but I can't deny that I'm affected by the vulnerability he's showing. Two months versus two weeks is a long time. However, I'm not as angry at Orion as I had been before our trip to Las Vegas. I'll concede to the fact that if that was his intention, to take me off for the weekend and work to change my mind, then his plan might have worked to a certain degree.

My sigh is laced with defeat. I pick up my cell phone and go to my notes. "I've made a list."

His eyebrows pull. "You made a list?"

"Of the gripes I have with you."

"You actually made a list?"

I blast him with my serious and unyielding glare. "You forced me to make a list. Number one," I read extra loudly. "I need you to show up to the office and to work every day of the work week."

He shakes his head, frowning. "I do that already."

"Wow. Talk about not being self-aware."

Orion throws his hands up. "I work every day."

"I don't see you every day."

His lips cut into the sexiest smirk. "You want to see me, Delilah?"

I roll my eyes. "Stop flirting. I'm serious."

He nods briskly. "Okay. Next."

"Yes?"

"It's a deal. Monday through Friday, you and me."

I force my eyes away from the way he's leering at me. I will not let that sexy look on his face distract me.

"Also…" I clear the frog out of my voice. "Juggle your own dates."

"I'm not dating anyone, so okay."

"You might want to check your calendar," I say with an eye roll. "And let me be clear, juggling your dates includes breaking your dates."

He sets his jaw. "Done. What else?"

"You drop off and pick up your own dry cleaning. I shouldn't know that you dry-clean your boxers." I shake my head swiftly. "Weird."

"It's not weird, Delilah. I like the way they feel after being dry-cleaned, and so does Gunther."

My finger shoots up because he just reminded me of something I forgot to put on my list. "Also, naming your penis. I don't want to know the name of your best buddy."

A mischievous gaze sits in Orion's eyes. "No Gunther—okay."

Release me...

My breaths are slow and hard as Orion's eyes hold me captive. My head is light as I experience a weird shadow effect of feeling his body against mine while his tongue strokes mine. The kiss is sensual, soft, and deep, and the memory so visceral.

"What are you thinking about, Delilah?" he asks.

I blink out of my daze to notice him smirking. "Nothing." I said that too fast and my voice was too high. My body is sizzling. *Did that really happen?* That couldn't have really happened...did it?

Orion grunts thoughtfully. "Anything else?"

My neck feels stiff as I nod while still trying to force that last memory from haunting me. It wants to come back but I won't let it. "It's time you do your own work."

He squishes his face as he shakes his head. "You

see, that's going to be my biggest ask of you. I'll need you to handle the reports while I perfect my AI software. The reports are bullshit, we both know it."

I yank my head back in surprise. Is that what he's been thinking about the work we do? "No, they're not," I say, shaking my head adamantly. "Your family needs to know the financial numbers to control spending, Orion. How can you not understand that?"

"They have departments full of people to do those reports, Delilah. They're fucking with me and in turn fucking with you."

"No," I cry.

"Yes."

"But I work so hard to extrapolate data for the reports. Those numbers are not easy to come by."

Orion slides two fingers across his kissable bottom lip as he ponders something. "Listen, I'll assist you with the reports from now on."

"Really?" I'm shocked that he offered. I always knew he felt compiling data was beneath him, and he just proved I was right. It's also not like Orion to engage in any task that he feels is beneath him, at least that's what I thought. I don't know anymore, maybe I haven't known very much about him at all.

"Okay," I squeeze out past my tight throat. "Thank you."

He winks at me. "You're welcome. And if I'm anything less than the best boss in the world, then by all means, call me out on my shit." He tilts his chin down and narrows an eye. "Deal?"

I nod tightly. "We have a deal."

CHAPTER 11

Lost and Found

TREASURE LORD

"**B**abe, I have to deal with this," Achilles grumbles.

"Uh-oh, what happened?" I ask.

My husband's eyes skim my body as I lay across the velvet chaise on my side with my hand propping up my head. We were moments away from christening this piece of very expensive furniture when he got a phone call. There are phone calls he ignores and then there those he takes. After every ring, a digital voice repeated 911, which meant he had to take the call.

"But first…" When Achilles gets up, his cock is at attention and aimed at me. I know what he must do first. We've been doing a whole lot of it lately, even before our wedding day. Can a couple have too much sex?

He stops. "What's wrong?"

I'm frowning as I gnaw on my lower lip, working out how to put what's on my mind into words. I think I got it.

I spiral my legs off the chaise to sit up. "I'm scared."

His frown deepens. "Scared of what?"

"That this is going to fizzle out one day."

"What?" he asks, leaning away from me yet remaining so close. "Sex?"

I nod gently.

"Ah, I see." He sounds equally relieved and compassionate of my feelings as he finishes walking to me and sits down beside me. "Of course, it will. We're newlyweds. And we've been fucking like crazy from the start. But, babe, that's okay because you and I are more than just fucking. I love you, and I like you, very much. You're a good time in and out of the bed." He ends with the sexiest smile ever.

"Aww..." I simper and then elbow him playfully in the arm. "I like you very much too."

We tumble into getting lost in each other's eyes. It's still so hard to believe that I fell in love with and married Achilles Lord. It's crazy how life works out.

"So, tell me…what was your call about?"

"Oh, not yet," he says and now Achilles is hovering over me. "On your knees." And to help me get into position he takes me by the hips and guides my ass up in the air.

POSTCOITAL AND SEXUALLY SATISFIED, WE HAVE moved back to the bed. I lay across Achilles's lap and we're watching his laptop screen as he plays one of several videos. He's told me that the house-maid found a diamond ring in the trash can in Orion's room. Hotel management had the serial code on the inside of the band checked and saw that it belonged to a woman named Delilah O'Shay and was purchased at the Temple of Love, a place where quick weddings are performed, in the wee hours of the morning on our wedding date. I laughed because if I ever pictured Orion ever settling down with one woman, it would be a scenario where he would be too drunk to know what he's doing. That's exactly what happened because we're looking at the scene play out on Achilles's screen. It's almost too comical to be true. And Delilah is totally out of it. I can't understand a word she's saying other than, "I love him so much." And eventually she says, "I do."

They're making out—no, that's not what it's called. They're sucking each other's face as if they have to do it to keep a meteor from slamming into the planet and destroying mankind. And then...

I gasp. "Oh my God." My mouth is caught open.

"What the fuck?" Achilles whispers in awe.

To cap off their wedding ceremony, Delilah takes off her panties, straddles Orion and they have sex on the front bench in the chapel. The officiant and others casually walk out of the room as if they've seen it all before.

Achilles closes his laptop. Speechless, we both look at each other.

Finally, I'm able to swallow and ask, "We have to go back to New York. You have to deal with this. They're married."

Achilles's features tighten as he ponders the situation. We're staying in a castle his family owns in Angus, Scotland. This is just the beginning of our honeymoon. We have three beautiful and solid weeks planned of traveling the world and making love from sun to sun.

"I don't think either of them remembers any of this shit. Kurt also told me that Orion knocked a guy out with one punch after the guy pulled a gun on him and attempted to steal his watch."

I gasp. "No?"

"Yes, babe. Yes."

I laugh so hard I almost pee and Achilles eventually joins me. This craziness we've just learned is insane. But eventually, Achilles decides to let them stay married since it won't be so easy for them to divorce. That deal we made, the one that brought Achilles and me together, is not set in stone yet— soon but not yet. The rules of the old Lord trust still apply. A quickie Vegas wedding, sex in the chapel, followed by an annulment will give a Lord heir not affiliated with Achilles's clan cause to challenge the deal they made with my family in a court of law. The Lord Family Trust purity clauses can do them in. And if that happens, they'll almost be back to square one. I say almost because my family will always have money, but the Lords will probably lose everything.

"Then you don't want them to get a divorce?" I ask Achilles when our laughter dies down.

"They should not get a divorce until the deal is set in stone."

"Ha," I say as a thought drops into my head. "I guess buying *Top Rag Mag* was the smartest move you made in recent history."

Achilles sweeps my curly hair off my shoulder and softly kisses my bare skin. "Marrying you was the smartest move I made in recent history," he says. "Buying *TRM* was the second smartest move. But, of course, that deal can all go to shit if my side of our family drops the ball. So…"

Achilles expertly guides me onto my back, positions his body between my thighs, and moves into me.

Squeezing the sheets, I gasp at first thrust.

"We can't drop the ball," he whispers in a shivering voice.

CHAPTER 12

DELILAH O'SHAY

I tried to add one more item to our deal, which would give us separate offices but Orion wouldn't cave. He said the smaller office has bad ventilation, but I don't believe him. I think he has a problem with sitting alone in a room—classic abandonment issues. Although, considering his relationship with his mother, brothers, and even his father, I can't say that would be the case. The reason he doesn't want to make separate work spaces for us surely can't be that he wants to sit around and look at me all day. It has to be something else.

Regardless, I let go of my ask for my own small office, at least for now. It's Friday. Orion and I have gotten through a whole week of working across from each other after our Vegas weekend. Orion has been on time every day for five days, which is a new record for him. On Tuesday and Thursday, he even arrived before I did. However, when I walked into the office, he wasn't at his desk but somewhere else in the building. I find myself feeling more peaceful when he's not sitting across from me. I've dreamed about him every single night this week, which can't be a good thing. I also avoid eye contact with him as much as possible. The good thing is my tasks have expanded past reports. Orion has given me these psychological quizzes to complete. Some of the quizzes have been over twenty pages long. Each question has to do with human nature, which I find interesting. Orion has told me to take my time to complete the quizzes, and by no means should I finish them after-hours or over the weekend. Then he graced me with a smile. Gosh he's too gorgeous for his own good.

I stop typing and gaze unfocused at his unoccupied desk while swiveling from left to right in my chair. I wonder what or who he's doing this weekend. I used to know which mountain he'd be climbing when I kept his calendar, but he's taken that off my plate too. Seven women have called the office hoping to reach him this week. In each case, I sent them directly to his voice mail. I'm hands-off when it comes to his private life. I thought I would love not knowing but not knowing is sort of driving me crazy.

Suddenly the office door opens swiftly and Orion steals my attention away from his desk.

"Lila, we're ready. Let's go," he says excitedly.

My cringing is only short-lived when he called me Lila. We've brokered a deal on him calling me Lila instead of Lilly. I gave him permission to use it for the whole week, and then on Monday we'll discuss him carrying on calling me that. I think I'll let him continue if he wants. He's been a good boss. If he wants to call me Lila, then I'll allow it.

"Go where?" I ask.

"To my domain."

"Your domain?"

He waves his head toward the hallway. "Let me show you."

"THE BASEMENT?" I ASK, GLARING AT HIM incredulously.

We're at the elevators and he smashed the B button for basement.

"Yes. The basement."

"Don't tell me…"

Orion laughs.

"No, Lila," he says with a laugh. "We're not there yet."

My eyebrows shoot up. "Don't talk that way. The goal is to go up, not down."

The elevator dings and the doors slide open.

Orion's arm is outstretched, keeping the door open so that I may enter first. "Oh, that's news to me."

"What's news to you?" I ask. I'm way too close to him as I walk inside the elevator.

"Are you admitting that you want me to take you to the penthouse floor with me? Because I will. Anything for you, Lila."

He's flirting, which means he's being an unserious asshole. My sigh is full of resolve. "I guess it's true what they say."

"What do they say?"

"A leopard never changes his spots and a flirt will forever live and die on his charm."

His shoulders shake when he chuckles. Even the way he does that is sexy. Why am I seeing sexy, sexy,

sexy, these days whenever I regard Orion? I don't like it.

"No one says that, Lila."

I sigh very hard as my hand flies up and I show him my palm. "Okay, you're overdoing the Lila."

Oh, that cunning smile is coupled with a lip lick. I want to kiss him. No—I want him to kiss me.

Ding. The door opens and Orion waits for me to exit first. The way his gaze lays over my face makes me feel flustered as I enter the hallway.

"You look nice today, Lila," he remarks.

I can feel his eyes on my backside before I turn to face him. "So do you." That slipped out.

But he does look really good today. His black pants have a little sheen to them that almost make them appear smoke gray. He has on a short-sleeved shirt that is the same color as his pants and the material lays over his chest and abdominal muscles like a soft kiss.

"Thank you—Lila," he says, lapping me up with a playful gaze.

I roll my eyes. "Whatever, Jack."

I barely registered that we were walking until we make it to the door at the end of the lonely hallway. No one ever comes down here, that's for sure. I'm surprised we haven't had a run-in with a rat. After all, this is New York City.

"Who's Jack?" Orion asks.

"If you can call me Lila, then I can call you Jack."

Orion tilts his head curiously. "Calling you Lila bothers you that much?"

Honestly? Not anymore. "Yes."

"Why?"

I shrug. "I don't know."

I start to feel a tiny bit uncomfortable as Orion stares at my face. It's as if he can tell that I'm not being 100 percent truthful. I'm actually being immature and I hate it.

He grunts thoughtfully as he puts his finger on a keypad and then opens the door. "After you."

I lift a foot to step inside but then put it back down. "It doesn't bother me," I admit. "Lila's fine."

It feels like the part of the movie when the hero and heroine kiss, but instead he's grinning at me and I'm flapping my eyelashes at him. Once again, I feel like telling him where I woke up on Saturday morning. I can't believe I've been keeping that to myself. I think he deserves to know.

My Orion problems tumble down the drain as

soon as I'm inside the room and see six large screens fixed to the wall, about sixty inches each. Three of them are filled with long lines of computer code. Two men sit at desks programming multiple computers.

"Sally, meet Lila," Orion says.

"Hello, Lila. Thanks for introducing us, Orion," a flawless female voice says.

Orion and I smile at each other, and to show him how proud of him I am, I wink at him too.

So far, I've had a conversation with Sally, Mike, and Ben, who actually sounds like Orion's friend Ben. Orion says he thought it was time Ben saw himself the way everyone sees him.

"Well," I say, "It's been well-documented that computers are more self-aware than humans."

Orion grunts thoughtfully. "That's why I brought you here."

"Because computers are more self-aware than I am?" I ask.

I'm glad he laughs softly. That was indeed a joke.

"Daniel, present to her the problem with cube

number forty-eight," Orion says to one of the programmers.

For the first time since I've arrived a very skinny man with dark hair and pale skin, someone who looks like they should be the last person cooped up in the basement with no vitamin D, stops typing to look at him. His eyebrows rise a fraction higher when our gazes meet.

"The problem is creating accurate sentience—" he starts.

"Well, that's because it can never occur with a computer," I say, cutting him off.

"I don't know about that," Daniel says.

"But a computer doesn't have blood. It doesn't have evolutionary cravings like hunger, thirst, sleep or lust." My thoughts on this topic flow smoothly and clearly. I've been thinking about this ever since Orion asked me to fill out the question-naires. I had a feeling they were trying to reach sentience with their AI software and that would definitely be the wrong path to take in my opin-ion. "You would have to program a machine with those needs in order to make your AI truly sentient."

"And why is that?" Orion asks. His arms are folded across his broad chest and eyebrows pinched, indicating that he's taking me very seriously. That's so attractive.

I nod first, realizing I'm on a roll and how good it feels to talk about one of my favorite subjects. "Take Darwinism itself. I've argued that it's an extreme reaction to religion—an extreme secular trope to counteract an extreme religious trope. And somewhere in the middle is the truth. That's where your AI software's strength should reside. I mean, why waste time trying to make a computer do what it will never be able to do? Do you want your software to actually be intelligent and not emotional? You're using it to sell products, right?"

Orion's thoughtful frown intensifies as he barely says, "Right."

"But," Daniel says extra fervently to claim the floor. "The goal is sentience."

"Then your goal is to create slaves." I can't believe I said that. But since I said it… "Humans want to create other humans they can dominate. People who say they believe in God don't really trust what they believe. And those who say they don't believe in God aren't seeing the evidence right in the mirror." I shake my head adamantly. "It's never going to happen, Orion."

"Then what do you suggest?" Orion asks before

Daniel can offer up a counterargument to what I just said.

"I suggest you make AI software that plays to a computer's strength, which is self-awareness. And then use that software to help make humans become more self-aware, which is a very difficult feat for our species."

Orion's lips are positioned to respond when my cell phone chimes and vibrates. By habit I put it in my skirt pocket before I walked out of the office. Also, by habit I've taken it out of my pocket to see that I just got a message from Xena asking if I want to go to lunch with her.

"How about we do lunch today," Orion asks, jutting his neck forward to read the message on my screen.

WE'RE EATING PIZZA AT ENZO'S, WHICH ISN'T FAR away from the office. I sit in the same office with the man all day long so I can't understand why I'm so nervous to be out in public having lunch with him. Maybe it's because almost everybody is looking at us. It has already dawned on me that I'm out in an ordinary restaurant with an extraordinary public figure. I keep forgetting that the Lords are like American royalty. Maybe because there's nothing extraordinarily uncommon about the family. They're just people.

"Listen," Orion starts and pauses, waiting for me to set my attention back on him.

I raise my eyebrows to let him know I'm listening.

"We haven't tried to work out that night we spent together in Las Vegas."

I'm so grateful I didn't swallow at that moment. I would've choked. "What's there to work out?"

Orion frowns and then evens out his expression a few times. Something is troubling him deeply. He checks over both shoulders and then leans his powerful shoulders across the table. "I woke up with no clothes on and my dick got some action."

"Got some action?" I feign surprise. I didn't know I was such a good little actress.

He shrugs and then sits back. "Gunther was sticky and pretty raw." He scratches his forehead nervously. "Those are signs that I had done a lot of fucking. I'm surprised the woman didn't stick around and claim her name to fame." He ends on a cocky smile.

I swallow the extra moisture that poured into

my mouth. How do I tell him that it was me he had sex with? I can also validate that my vagina had lingering evidence that it had experienced a lot of sex that night too. I just don't understand why I can't remember any of it. It's been a week. I haven't consumed a drop of alcohol since that night, and didn't even drink champagne at the wedding. *Why can't I remember?*

"Um, well...maybe you slept with Heather," I offer up.

He taps his finger on the tabletop. "Heather arrived that morning. Plus, I would know if it was her."

"Really?"

"Yes."

"How?"

Orion's grin makes me grin too.

"What?" I ask.

"I know you don't think highly of me, but you've never heard me speak of my sexual conquests."

My head whips into a side tilt. "Is that what she is? A sexual conquest?"

"All sex is conquest," he retorts.

We stare into each other's eyes. I can't help but wonder how the drunk Delilah O'Shay liked sex with Orion Lord. I bet he can really make a girl arrive at climax.

Orion's amused gaze dances around my face. "You're thinking."

"I'm always thinking," I say.

"About me?"

I shake my head even though he's exactly who's on my mind.

"But you don't think we…?" He turns his head sightly as if that look on his face is finishing his question for him.

"I…" *Do not hyperventilate, Lilly.*

"Because I left the party with you, and I can't imagine finding a stranger to fuck between leaving you and waking up the next morning."

"You can't?" My pitch was too high. I have to get control of myself.

"No. Contrary to what you believe about me, Lila. I don't frivolously fuck around. As I said, I'm a conquistador."

I shake my head. "What does that even mean?"

He rubs his chin, stretching his neck as I wait for him to explain himself. But then he stops stroking his chin and sits still for a few seconds studying me.

My breaths are uneven. I so very much want to

ask what is he thinking. Does he remember something? Maybe he wasn't as drunk as I was. I've researched my condition already. My memories of being with him are lost forever.

"So, how has your week been?" he asks, picking up a slice of pizza and biting into it.

Oh God, I'm relieved as I focus on his perfect mouth. I've been told my mouth is perfect too. We had to have kissed if we had sex. I bet kissing him was like a drug.

I drop my gaze and clear my throat. "Are you inquiring about your performance as my new and improved boss?"

He chuckles. "I've improved?"

I can look at him again and so I do. "Very much so." I'm simpering.

"Happy to hear it. Since your weekend is unencumbered by me, do you have any dates lined up?"

A lot goes through my head as I try not to let my expression show the cards I'm now playing. For some reason, I wish I could say that I have a hot date planned for the weekend because I want to see his reaction. But I'm already lying to him even as I sit here in silence. "Nope," I say, taking a bite of my pizza. "You?"

He sets down his half-eaten pizza slice and

presses his back against his chair. "Only a family obligation."

"Oh, that sounds fun."

"It depends," he says, frowning and then shifts abruptly in his seat. "Anyway, I like what you said earlier about AI and sentience. It's definitely human to shove square pegs into round holes, isn't it?"

I laugh, welcoming the change of subject. "Definitely."

Orion and I discuss the idea of AI being more superior than humans and how that can benefit LTI. It's nice having a real professional and adult conversation with him. For the first time ever, we've officially entered a period of getting along.

"Wait," Orion says out of the blue. He's glaring at my chin.

Like watching a car crash in progress, I observe his finger moving toward my face. His finger lands on my chin and swipes left. "You had cheese on your chin."

My mouth is stuck open and my heart is beating like a drumline. The time has come to officially admit that I have become sexually attracted to Orion Lord. And now that I'm being honest with myself, it's time to become unsexually attracted to Orion Lord. He's not good for me. He said it himself, women are conquests for him. He's still a fuckboy, which is why I fucked him while drunk.

So, I close my mouth and smile warmly at him. If we can't be lovers or remain boss and employee for longer than two months max, then maybe we can become friends. "Thank you," I say.

He winks. "You're welcome, Lila."

CHAPTER 13

Results

ORION LORD

Friday night goes by in a blur. I'm attending a Lord Foundation charitable benefit. My mother strongly suggested that I be Heather's date. Heather looks stunning tonight as usual. She's a beautiful woman but she and I are like fire and ice. I'm the fire. She has the ability to freeze a lake of lava. We move around the room, shaking hands, thanking guests for their contributions. Everybody believes we're a real couple. I know better than to correct them. My mother wants us to leave that impression on donors. In Marigold's eyes, Heather would be the perfect daughter-in-law. Her family has lots of money and connections, and as my mother said, "Heather can throw one hell of a fundraiser." She also thinks Heather will improve my bad reputation.

People think Achilles runs our family but he doesn't. Marigold is the true puppet master, and my brothers and I know it. That's definitely why I'm being a good son tonight. However, I can't get Delilah off my mind. I see her face even when I'm trying not to. I do remember kissing the top of her head in the back of the car. I also recall dancing with her and then we kissed again. She has to remember some of that, but she's pretending not to. Is being with me that much of a problem for her?

We had to have fucked. Before driving to Heather's house to pick her up for our date, I made a call to the hotel. Our suites were on the VIP floor where there were cameras. They had to have been working due to the guests that were being housed for the weekend. I asked for security, told them who I was. Manuel, security chief of the hotel, said I had called just in time. The hotel wipes security footage from the previous week every Saturday at midnight. He said he'll search the footage and get back to me if he finds something.

I'd been distracted all night waiting for that call. He probably won't find anything.

My eyes catch sight of two people I really don't

want to see tonight. "Shit," I say under my breath. Here they come.

"O," Mina calls with her sister in tow. The twins rarely do anything apart.

"Mina," I say. We hug and then I hug Lina too.

They both smile at Heather. The twins don't like her and she doesn't care for them.

"I thought you'd show up with your new squeeze," Mina says. "What's her number anyway?"

"I have it," Lina replies.

This fucking moment is moving too fast for me to keep up. "Who the hell are you talking about?"

"Lilly," Lina replies.

They think she's my new squeeze? "Lila is my assistant."

Lina elbows Mina. "Mina's been having fantasies about turning her."

I frown. "Turning her?"

The twins chuckle as my cell phone rings. Frowning at them, I look to see who it is.

"You might want to put that away," Heather whispers, looking at my cell phone as if scolding it.

The twins raise their eyebrows at each other. They don't have to speak, I can tell that they're saying, "See, she's mean-mommy-girlfriend." That's what they call her.

But I recognize the number on my screen. It's a 7-0-2 area code.

"I have to take this," I say, walking away from the ladies with my phone against my ear.

"I THINK TONIGHT WENT WELL, DON'T YOU?" Heather says.

She's sitting next to me in the back seat of my chauffeured limousine. I haven't been paying attention to much of what she's been saying. Heather mentioned how much money the foundation raised tonight, but the amount won't be confirmed until the final tally. Someone very important, according to her, invited us to dinner on Sunday night.

"Orion, are you listening to me?" she asks.

Not really. "A little," I say.

"I really think we should have a sound talk about you and me. Especially since people are starting to talk."

I've been irritated ever since Manuel sent me video of early Saturday morning of last week. I'm not upset with Delilah about the first part of the security footage. We were both fucked-up. I do however blame her for what happens right before 7:00 a.m. After I got the video, I found a quiet place and watched it four times back-to-back. We fucked in the hallway next to my suite. And no one caught us. I had Delilah against the wall. I entered her with ease. She held on to me and we made out as I humped until I came—inside her. Fuck. I always use a condom. I just wish I could remember that shit. I want to remember how she feels around my cock. I looked like I was experiencing bliss. I kept repeating something. I think it was how good she felt. *Fuck!*

"Earth to Orion," Heather says, snapping her fingers.

I close my eyes as I sigh and then massage my temples. "Not tonight, Heather."

"Then when?"

"You're not my girlfriend," I snap.

"But for our purposes..."

"What purposes?"

She sighs as if I'm annoying her. "You're a Lord and I'm a Van Buren. We have obligations to our families. Hell, to the world."

I look at her, searching for a break in her mask. I want to know if she's fucking with me. She's not.

"It's 2022. What kind of fucking obligations do we have to our families who for the majority part are coke-heads, criminals, and lazy-ass and entitled pricks?"

She gasps as if I just slapped her across the face.

The car stops right on time. "We've arrived," Ellis's voice projects through the back seat speakers.

"Is that what you think of my family and me?" Heather roars.

She hasn't moved an inch and I really need her to get the fuck out already. I check my watch. It's six minutes after midnight. That's still early in these parts.

"Do you have somewhere to go?" she asks.

"Actually, I do."

"Another woman."

"Yes. Another woman."

Heather is so silent that I'm forced to look at her. The expression on her face is odd; it's earnest.

"You know I don't care about that. You can fuck who you want to fuck. But I want to wear the ring."

My eyes constrict as I watch her. I'm having a visceral reaction to her. It's odd. It's as if she's damn familiar. She's the embodiment of what I've been trying to avoid for my entire life. I thought it had worked, but here I'm sitting in the car with it, her, my fucking fear. How did that happen?

"Good night, Heather," I eventually say.

She still doesn't move. I don't like getting aggressive with women. It's not my style.

Her door opens and Ellis is standing beside it waiting for her to step out. If looks could kill, I'd be dead.

Heather shakes her head and, after a shivering sigh, says, "We're not done."

The only reason I don't say that we are done is because of that one part she mentioned earlier— obligation. Not until tonight have I accepted that Heather Van Buren has up until now been my unspoken obligation. But right now, I can't process that part of my life. I play the video on my phone again and watch myself fuck Delilah. She's on my mind, and she's the person that I need to hash things out with.

CHAPTER 14
Sober

DELILAH O'SHAY

T onight, I had dinner with Xena, Tabitha,
and Sarah. Sarah and Tabitha are
dancers. I think Xena invited them to
dinner with us so that I can remember what's
important. All night I had to hear about all the
shows they've danced in since their careers took off.

"You don't want to sit out too long, Lilly,"
Tabitha said, flipping her long jet-black hair from
hanging across one shoulder to the other. That's a
habit of hers. My guess is that it's a biological
tendency. People have those. "What we do is so
taxing on the body. You cannot be out of shape."
Her eyes quickly examined me, judging my physical
condition.

I didn't say anything in my defense. I know I'm not

in pristine dancer's condition. But I'm still a better dancer than she is. And I don't want to be bony and muscular. I rather like my softer body. After my conversation with Orion earlier in the day, I'd been thinking about going to graduate school and getting my master's degree in psychology rather than dancing.

"Oh, she's still got it," Xena said. "She's going to quit her job in two months and leave that asshole boss of hers in Christmas past, right, Lilly?"

I smiled tightly at her at first. "Why do you hate Orion so much?" I asked. "Because you barely even know him."

"I know a lot about him, actually. You've been bitching and moaning about him for four and a half years."

Oh…right, I thought. *That's how she knows him.*

Eventually, I made it home. I hadn't been able to sleep. That's why I got out of bed and made myself a slice of croissant toast with strawberry jelly. I've also made the decision to tell Orion about waking up in his bed and about the ring I was wearing come Monday morning. He deserves to know the truth.

Leaning against the counter, I finish my last bite of toast. I hadn't eaten much tonight, Tab's and

Sarah's talk about being in shape and all of their gigs stole my usually hearty appetite. I really don't care about gaining weight. I'd like to stay healthy but skinny can go right to the hell it takes to maintain such a weight.

My doorbell buzzes and I immediately look at the time on the microwave.

"Who the hell is that?"

Instead of answering it, I rinse the butter knife I used to spread jelly. I think it's someone who got the wrong apartment number. They'll figure it out and go away. At least that's what I thought until the bell buzzes again, followed by knocking.

I race over to the door and look through the peephole.

Jerking back, I gasp. "Orion?"

"It's me. Open up. I have to show you something."

I CAN STILL FEEL THE NIGHT COMING OFF HIM AS I watch him fucking me against the wall on his phone. It's as if my consciousness has left my body on one hand. On the other hand, my pussy is tingling like crazy. Maybe it's muscle memory that's taking place down there.

"Wow," I say breathlessly.

Orion swallows audibly. "Keep watching."

I'm forced to glance at him, since his tone is rather cold. He comes inside me. Fuck. No condom. I could be pregnant for all I'm concerned.

"Fuck," I mutter.

"My sentiments exactly."

What is he so mad about? He scored!

But then the next scene plays out at 6:48 a.m. The door to his suite opens.

"Oh no," I whisper.

"Oh yes."

I already know the rest because I lived it, which is why I hand him back his phone.

ORION AND I SIT ON MY SOFA STARING AT whatever's on the wall. I don't know about him, but I'm looking at the television I rarely watch. After outing me for creeping out of his room after waking up in his bed, he couldn't just leave. There's a lot that needs to be discussed.

"Sorry," I say yet again.

He slowly shifts his focus from whatever he's been staring at to me. "When were you going to tell me?"

"Monday." I say that with such conviction because even though I made that promise to myself, I had changed my mind right before the doorbell rang. "Well, maybe not. I probably would've chickened out by then."

"But I told you I woke up knowing I had sex with somebody and you couldn't tell me it was you?"

I sigh, fall back against the sofa, and press my folded forearms over my eyes. "I wanted to. It's not like I can remember us having sex because I don't."

Orion is silent for far too long. I remove my arms to see what's going on with him. He's staring at my pebble-nippled breasts. Okay so, just sitting here with him after watching that video has made me horny, but I'll get over it as soon as he leaves.

He licks his bottom lip as a sultry gaze comes to his eyes. "I want to remember it, Lila. That's why I'm here." His eyebrows flash up suggestively.

The way he's looking at me is saying something. I think I understand the language he's speaking, but it seems so unreal. "You're here to remember sex with me?"

"I want to remember it," he says so low that it's almost a whisper.

"Oh." My lips are stuck in the O position as his hands run up my bare thigh. I'm wearing my pajama-short set tonight.

I can't take my eyes off his large, warm hand traveling up my thigh. His touch feels sensual and I'm so turned on that I'm already sucking air.

"Are you sober, Delilah?" he asks.

"Yeah," I say tightly. "Are you?"

"Very."

His fingers are up over the band of my shorts. "Relax," he soothingly says as his hand maneuvers. We don't take our eyes off each other. But his skin is against my skin and I'm shivering. Orion is shivering too that's why I'm not embarrassed. We're in this together.

"Oh," I cry out as he touches my hot spot. I cling to his arms as Orion Lord rubs, and rubs, and rubs.

"Umm," he moans as if he's feeling exactly what I'm feeling. My body tenses as pleasure builds, and builds, and... "Fuck." He takes my shorts by both sides and tugs them down over my legs. His eyes are possessed by fire and desire as he falls to his knees and curls his muscular arms around my thighs. I slide down and my upper back pinches the sofa cushion as he tugs my clam to his mouth.

"Ohh…" I whimper as a soft and warm force stimulates me.

A few licks and I'm already on the verge of coming. I try to sink my fingers into my sofa cushions, but they're too firm to latch on to.

"Oh my…" The sensation builds one brick at a time. I suck air, on the way to losing my shit. I have to see. How is he able to do that?

"Mmm…" he groans.

And then my body tightens… "Ah-ah-ah-ah-ah," I cry as my sex quivers and luxuriates with orgasm.

"That was quick," Orion says after my orgasm subsides and I'm breathing heavily, trying to catch my breath. His devilish grin is going to be the end of me.

I'm lost for words even though there's so much to say. Here he is, Orion Lord, on his knees and he just made me come with his mouth. What the hell is happening?

"We're going to do this next part slow, Delilah, nice and slow."

HE'S TAKEN MY HAND AND WALKED ME TO MY bedroom. He's unbuttoned my pajama top, one latch at a time while gazing into my eyes. Finally, I know how it feels to have Orion's lips kissing mine and I know the taste and feel of his tongue. Through our kissing, I find myself whimpering like a lost puppy. His body is made of steel. He's strong. His arms are around me and I am putty in his hands.

"I knew you would taste sweet, Delilah," he whispers against my moistened lips. His breath feels deliciously warm. "Soft too."

Orion's tongue plummets deep into my mouth. My head feels buoyant and so does my body—so does this moment. My senses are blowing their top as his mouth consumes my right breast and then my left. My legs shiver, sex throbs, and I hear myself saying his name, pleading for more.

"It's time," he says.

We stare into each other's eyes as I help him lift the hem of his shirt. Once we arrive at the top of his chiseled chest, he takes it from there. I plant a kiss on his smooth skin. Orion is a work of art, carved by a master.

"Lie down and relax," he says, nodding his chin at the bed. "I'm going to do all the work."

Do all the work? I'm not sure I can let him do all the work. Look at his body. I want to clamor to get my hands and my mouth on him.

What's wrong with you, Lilly? He's still a fuckboy. Yes, he is. But I must let the fuckboy fuck himself out of my system. That's why I don't look away as he unbuttons and then unzips his pants.

I gasp and my eyes expand at the sight of his cock.

"You like it?" he asks.

I swallow and then nod. It's not too large. And it certainly isn't small. The skin on his cock is soft, perfect. The head glistens.

"I want you in my mouth," I say, reaching for his cock.

"No, baby. You want me exactly where I'm going." He finishes rolling a condom over his manhood and now, here he comes, moving over my body. "I'm going to make you come your brains out."

My knees separate. His weight is on top of me. Orion moves inside me and I gasp.

"HOLY FUCK," I SAY TIGHTLY. MY THIGHS ARE shivering, again an orgasm races through my pussy. His previous pump made me arrive. When I stiffened and screamed, and he felt my walls shiver around him, he held still, prolonging the sensation. I'm not surprised Orion expertly knows his way around a vagina. *Fuck.* He has the power to make me an addict for him. No wonder those women kept coming back for more. He's the ultimate fuck.

Orion rolls me on top of him and I lay on his body like a rag doll. I'm all out of steam. Our bodies glisten with sweat and I can hardly keep my eyes open. No wonder he said he'll do all the work.

"This…what we did…wasn't ordinary," I'm able to get out.

Orion chuckles. "I'm glad you liked it."

I want to say I more than liked it. I just experienced the most enjoyable activity I've ever partook in. I want to say that I loved it a hundred times over. But I know better than to use the word *love* in this situation. I also know better than to geek out outwardly about his golden dick.

"Well, at least we got that out of our systems, right?" I say with a tired smile.

I feel him stiffen beneath me. "It looked like we were getting it out of our system in Vegas."

"Yeah… You were really nailing me against that wall, and without a condom too," I say with a laugh.

"If it comes to it, then we'll have to do the right thing."

My eyebrows shoot up. I can hardly believe he went there. I'm working overtime to keep my cool. "And what's the right thing?"

He's silent for a few seconds. "You know what the right thing is."

I do know what the right thing is, but I'm wondering, are we talking about the same "right thing."

"Shit," he finally mutters. "My dick is sore like it was last week. We overdid it again." He points to the bathroom. "I'll be right back."

Orion rolls me off him as if I'm as light as a cotton ball on his chest. I think that's my favorite thing about him, his strength. I've never been with such a powerhouse of a man.

"Hey," he calls from the bathroom.

"Yep." I try to sound cool and unemotional, but for some reason I feel like crying.

"How about I stay over tonight? So, we can do it again in the morning?"

I quietly gasp as I pump my fist victoriously.

"Sure. Okay," I say as if it's no big deal, expertly hiding the fact that I'm over the moon.

THERE ARE SOME MEN A GIRL HAS SEX WITH FOR the first time and afterward she knows things will never be the same. You know you're in for a ride and you just pray that the road is smooth. In the spooning state, that's how I feel right now. Hopefully, I'll have more clarity in the morning.

I yawn. "Good night, Orion."

When he says, "Good night, Lila," his breath tickles the skin on my back. "Oh, and the right thing would be to marry of course." His sensual lips plants a soft kiss on the back of my shoulder.

Staring into the dark room I don't know whether to smile or panic. Now is the time to tell him about the ring.

"What do you think about that?" he asks.

Tell him.

I chuckle nervously. "I think you're hopped up on those male sex hormones."

His solid body shakes against me. "Maybe. Maybe not."

"We'll just have to see in the morning," I say with a laugh.

Orion yawns, kisses my back again, and that's how we leave it.

Orion did move inside me before the sun came up. Two big, strong hands cupping my breasts, he thrusted into me sensually, indulgently. I had the best orgasm ever. But what I felt was more than just physical. Tears pooled in my eyes. My heart felt so full that it ached. I did not say it out loud, but I swallowed those three scary words before I could say them out loud, scary because they are never to be uttered to your scoundrel of a boss. I'm thinking about that moment right now and thanking my lucky stars that I never said those words. Because it's Saturday morning and I'm in bed alone. He left without telling me.

I'm fully awake. The muted sun spills through the window. I flop an arm out to the space Orion has left empty and sigh. Staring at the ceiling, I will admit this, but only to myself, my bed has never felt so big and empty.

I'm ready for real love. I know that now. Being

with Orion has opened up something inside me, something real and inviting, and lasting. That acceptance has filled my heart with bliss. It's odd, but it has. I sit up. I'm not drowsy. I'm not sad. I'm ready to enjoy my first weekend that Orion will not be bothering me with his personal nonsense, nor any more sex.

CHAPTER 15
A New Pact

DELILAH O'SHAY

O rion is totally out of my system. And I
can say that with a cool head. Yes, the
sex was astronomically enjoyable. I'll
probably never do it with someone who has such a
gift for giving a girl orgasms. But sex is a very small
portion of what makes a relationship work. I refuse
to be "dickmatized" by the likes of Boss Scoundrel.

It was my dad just being himself who
reminded me how a man should make me feel
before I truly take him seriously. I took the
subway to my parents' townhome in Brooklyn
Heights. They asked me to come over right away,
my dad had something to show me. My heart
swelled for the five minutes my father ran on his
treadmill. After his accident, the doctors told

him that he had less than a one percent chance he'd ever walk again. But the expensive rehabilitation center that my mom and I had put all of my disposable cash into helped him beat those odds.

I clapped so hard my palms stung. Then my dad made another big presentation where he awarded me back all the money I had put into his treatment. The settlement for the accident came through and now my parents are multimillionaires. I didn't want the money, of course.

"But, sweetheart," he said. "I heard you were leaving your job. I know you kept working there for me. Use the money to help fund what you want for yourself."

And just so I couldn't absolutely insist on not taking the money, my parents had already transferred the funds into my account. So now, I'm independently rich, sort of. I'm not Lord or Grove rich, but I now have options. It's Monday morning, the start of a new week. I'm sitting at my desk and if I weren't such a woman of my word, I would pack my desk up and leave this job forever.

"Good morning," Orion says as he whisks into the office almost like Kramer on Seinfeld. "Did you get my message?"

I got his message, although I hadn't looked at it until last night.

I start typing up last week's expense report. Before he entered, I was daydreaming.

"Yes. You're sorry you had to leave. Your apology is accepted. And by the way, let's just call it one and done." My fingers type just as forcefully as my sigh. "We'll just get back to sanity." I stop typing and smile at him. My face hurts.

"I had fun on Friday night," he says as he sits on the edge of his desk.

I try to decipher the energy and face that he's giving me. My intuition is warning me not to fall for whatever he's serving.

"Me too."

"I was thinking..." The door opens and in walks the sound of sprightly high heels tapping against the floor.

"Good morning." Heather sweeps past my desk and stops directly in front of Orion. "You left these at dinner last night."

I force my jaw to stay put. I will not let myself frown either. I get back to work as whatever she gives Orion jingles. It sounds like keys.

"I told you I would pick them up later," he grumbles.

"I was in the neighborhood and Rodolpho knows me so I didn't have a problem getting past the guard. Hi, Delilah."

I halt the feverish speed of my typing and look up at her. Her fake smile is very pretty. The two of them standing together present as the perfect rich and snobby couple.

"Hello, Heather, good morning," I say.

Her smile slowly shrinks to nothing as she cuts her eyes away from me. That one act is saying you're not worth more attention than I've already given you. I want to get up and run out of the office and leave the two of them alone. But that savors too much like wound-licking.

"So, tonight, I was thinking you should pick me up at seven," she says.

The numbers on my computer are beginning to merge into each other. I'm fuming for so many fucking reasons.

"Seven…" Orion pauses. I know he's checking that damn watch of his.

I spring to my feet. "Going to the ladies' room, O." Yes, I called him O. I would say more but not in front of Heather. I've already given her the satisfaction of knowing that she has gotten to me just by making me walk out of my place of work.

I feel dizzy as I pad down the hallway. I don't have to go to the ladies' room. Instead, I ride up to the fourth floor to buy coffee. The line is long as usual. But I don't mind waiting. I have a lot of cooling off to do. I have to be my own shrink in this situation. Orion Lord is not the man for me. Sure, he gave me an apology, but he's not bursting at the seams to make me feel special. No…he wants to treat me like his other dames. He wants me to be happy with a kernel of his attention while he comes and goes as he pleases. That's not good enough for me.

"Hey, Lila!" Colby, one of the baristas, calls from behind the register.

I look around to make sure he's talking to me. He's looking right at me, so yes, I'm the Lila or Delilah in the room that he's addressing.

I step out of the line and walk to the front. "Yeah?" I'm so unsure why he called me to the front. Has Orion tracked me down?

"How are you doing this morning?" he asks, handing me a sixteen-ounce cup of something.

"What's this?"

"Your regular."

"My regular?"

"Vanilla bean latte with a dusting of chocolate powder under the foam."

I shake my head, confused as hell. "But why?"

"It's your boss. We've been told that as soon as you walk through the door, we're to make your order. If you want your order changed, then call us and let us know ahead of time."

I'm still processing this new perk that I have.

"It doesn't hurt working directly for Orion Lord, does it?" Colby says.

Oh, it hurts, Colby. It hurts a lot.

WHEN I MAKE IT BACK TO MY DESK WITH MY LATTE, Orion is on the phone. He tells whoever he's speaking to that he'll call them back just as I sit at my desk.

"Enjoy the wait?" he asks, sounding and looking proud of himself.

"Thank you," I say. My tone is professional.

"And listen, about Heather…"

"Nope," I say, raising a finger. "You don't have to explain."

"But I want to explain."

"Nope," I say again, shaking my head adamantly. "It's your personal business, Orion."

"Orion and not O?" he asks, grinning. What a perfect set of teeth he has—clean, pearly white, and straight. That smile of his is such a perfect little mouse trap.

"Sorry about that."

"Call me what you like," he croons seductively.

Of course, he'll flirt. He'll also fuck me. He's laying out the cheese. "No. I'll refer to you as Orion. And, really, let's forget about Friday night. Yes. It was fun for me too." My fake smile feels like it's going to swallow my whole head. "I got it out of my system, and whew…" I fold my shoulders forward, loosening my back. "I'm over it. I don't want sex from you anymore. No more sex."

Why in the world is he smirking?

"Then no more sex it is." He's still smirking.

"I mean it, Orion. Just work."

"I thought we were working on being friends?"

My lips are quivering again. That's because I want to blast his ass out and call him on this mind-fuck he's trying to put on me.

I square my shoulders and look him dead in the eye. "You're my boss and I'm your employee. How about we get through this part of our relationship first?"

Orion frowns thoughtfully, rubbing his palms together. "We had a family dinner last night to discuss foundation business. Heather was invited because she works with the foundation. Fifi, my mother's bichon frise who is in love with me"—he smiles, full of himself—"jumped in my lap and made me spill wine on my pants. I took my keys out while Marta, the housemaid, treated the stain for me. She likes me too."

I roll my eyes. "You're so full of yourself. You have a problem, Orion. And I fell into your trap once. And now that I'm out, I'd be a fool to go back for more."

He throws his hands up as though he's totally confused. "What did I say? I'm explaining to you what happened."

I shake my head. He doesn't even hear himself. "You need women to fall in love with you, even Fifi. I mean, that's why you're an expert at fucking. You thought you can make me come hard and then I'd be putty in your hands." This is so cathartic for me. I'm on a roll and now it's time to give him the punch line. The one that has been repeating itself over and over in my head like a broken record. "A vibrator can do what you do, honey. And I don't have to put up with its lack of respect!" I breathe deeply, catching my breath after that tirade.

His eyebrows ruffle and he tilts to one side and then the other as if chewing on every word I spoke. "You think I'm an expert at fucking?"

I jerk my head back. Although, I'm not surprised he asked me that. "Mr. Lord, did you send me a new set of psychological quizzes for the AI software?" That was an aggressive change of the subject and I'm proud of myself for it. My expression remains as stoic as a nun's on Sunday morning. I'm not letting him charm me into breaking the ice queen I have summoned from somewhere deep inside me.

"Okay, Lila, I'm your boss. We're kind of friends, almost friends. And no more of my expert fucking."

I don't break. "Exactly. And the AI quiz?"

Orion snorts a chuckle. "I would like it by the end of the day."

I nod dutifully. "You'll have it by the end of the day." I set my full attention on my computer screen. "Just let me finish this report first."

"Don't worry about the reports, Lila. I'll handle them. I want you on the AI quizzes, Lila."

I can't believe him. Two Lila's in a row. He's fucking with me, and still, I don't break.

"Thank you, O."

He chuckles. "You're welcome, Lila."

"Jerk."

"A jerk who's an expert at fucking."

Shit. I broke. But now, I'm back. I don't even respond. I get to work on the quizzes and he's back on his phone call.

CHAPTER 16

Definitely, Maybe

DELILAH O'SHAY

It's Friday and we've gotten through another entire week being professional with each other. Sure, Orion's gotten too close as he sat at my desk to go over the quiz and discuss AI business. I've also given him plenty of compliments about getting the reports ready on time. He still thinks the reports are bullshit. Whether they are or not, he completes them all in record time. I think Orion is an undercover genius. People with his sort of ability can go unnoticed in families like his. Hercules and Achilles have always been the stars of the Lords. Orion has been known as the blatant playboy with zero aspirations. The work he's doing with AI software is groundbreaking and he doesn't need a whole team of people to get it done. His team consists of Daniel, Hyun, Vic, and now me.

What's funny though is I'm toiling less but working harder. As I close down my computer to head out for the weekend, I stop to take a look at Orion. I'm surprised he's still here. Not only is he here though, he's working. He's a fast and precise typist. I've gotten used to the sound of his finger strokes. Not since our new pact have I really listened to his typing.

"Big date tonight?" I ask. I want to take that question back just as fast as I asked it.

"Nope," he says without looking away from his computer screen. "You?"

"Nope." But I am going to a party. No use in letting him know that part. My computer is powered all the way down. I collect my purse out of my bottom desk drawer. "Well…" I stand up. "See you on Monday."

Finally, Orion stops looking at his computer screen. My nipples stiffen as his gaze drops down and up my body. I know he still wants to bed me. I want to bed him too. But that kind of relationship between us is way too impractical. As he sits back in his chair, grinning in his charming way, I remind myself that he's the trap, that grin and the sensual way he just regarded me is the cheese, and I'm the mouse.

"Maybe I, um, can call you at—"

"Nope," I say, cutting him off. I'm heading to the door so fast, I might have left my shadow behind.

I make my escape fast. I can't hear whatever he wanted to say. I've been strong all week long. And he has been looking and smelling really delicious. I've even dreamed about him on Monday night, and Wednesday night, and then again on Thursday. The willpower I've been utilizing to resist him has so many cracks in the shield, it's close to shattering. So, no, I cannot hear what he has to say about getting together at some point this weekend.

I know I'm home free and safe from his mouse trap when my feet hit the New York City concrete and I'm on my way home. But just in case he decides to make it hard on me, I pick up my pace and make it home fast.

I SPEND FRIDAY NIGHT WITH XENA, AND TWO PEOPLE who have been friends of ours since childhood, Carol and Natalie. We drink cocktails and fill up on appetizers at the Blue Cherry. I have Shirley Temple cocktails. After what happened in Vegas, I just might stay away from alcohol for the rest of my life. I'm that way. One bad experience with something could turn me off that thing forever. But I'm having a fun night with friends. I feel like myself again, back before I started working for a high-maintenance boss that I had sex with last Friday night.

My attention falls on Xena as she laughs after Carol, who's a librarian, said she used a stapler as a weapon to stop a kid who was stealing books to sell on the internet. She notices me watching her intently. I haven't told her that I devoured the poisonous apple in a big way. She would probably insist that I quit working for Orion right this very second if I spilled the beans.

"Lilly, tell them about Vegas," Xena says to my surprise.

I have a feeling she's fishing for my thoughts. My cousin knows when I'm hiding something from her, and I suspect that she suspects it has something to do with Vegas and Orion.

But I welcome the challenge. I go into detail about my lavish hotel suite and all the famous people present. I tell them I danced with Lynx

Grove. The biggest reveal is that he's Mr. Eleventh Floor. Carol slaps her hand over her mouth as she gasps and Nat says, "No way?" so loud that the people at the next table whip their full attention in our direction.

"He likes you?" Nat asks. "Because if he does, then you should book it. Like, right this very second. What are you doing sitting here? Go book that shit."

I laugh because she's right but then I'm forced to reveal that he's in love with someone else. My friends groan in disappointment, even Xena, who already knows what happened between me and Lynx.

"But we're friends."

"He's a good friend to have," Carol says and points at each of us and continues, "You can get a professional athlete, and so can you, and you"—she stabs herself in the chest with her index finger—"and me."

"Well, not me," Xena says sheepishly.

Nat raises her hand, the back of it facing us. "Me neither."

It takes us a moment to get that she's flashing her diamond. One look at her sparkling ring puts a sick feeling in my stomach. I probably shouldn't have thrown mine in the trash can. What was I thinking?

On Saturday morning, I go walking with Hope, a friend I hadn't seen since forever, and then we do brunch. We talk about everything that happened in our lives since we last saw each other, which was nearly three years ago. Before I can slip a forkful of hash browns into my mouth my cell phone rings. I glance at the screen intending to let it go to voice mail, but the name on the screen catches me so far off guard that I tell Hope I have to take this.

I say "Hello?" to the caller, sounding confused about why the person is reaching out to little ole me.

10:03 P.M.

The party started an hour and three minutes ago. I paced in front of my apartment door from nine to nine thirty, fully dressed in a black silk slip dress and a pair of open-toe black heels that have straps that wrap around my ankles and calves. I was wary about coming, but it was like hearing the tower bell sound off in my head when I opened my door and made my way to Mina's party.

And I must say that I look really tempting tonight. I'm just having one of those nights when my looks are falling into the right places. The humidity has made my hair fluff out in a way that makes me look like I've just had sex. My lips are red, skin dewy. I'm not certain if Orion's here. I should've asked Mina if she had invited him. If she would've said yes, then for the sake of not tempting myself to have sex with him again, I would've stayed home.

Gazing up at the large iron front doors of Mina's townhome, I sigh. No, I wouldn't have stayed home. But what if Orion's here and he brought Heather with him?

"I should've asked," I whisper.

But I won't turn back now. As I walk up the steps, the doors swing open. I'm sprayed by the beats of pop rap music mixed with chatter. I like this kind of music. It's the sort that instantly pumps sex appeal and self-esteem through my body. I don't know why I'm so nervous. Maybe it has to do with Mina and the social circle I'm entering. If it weren't for accompanying Orion to the wedding, I would've never met the twins. And their crew is Orion's crew. Gosh, I hope I don't run into him tonight.

The music is pretty prominent inside. The fact that you can't hear any of it while outside standing on the porch is also indicative of how much money they have. It must've cost an arm and a leg to soundproof this place. I'm on the Upper East Side. I don't know the neighborhood. I gave the cab driver the address and he brought me. But the nearby mini-mansions also smell of money.

I'm catching the eyes of the partygoers as I journey deeper into the residence. A beautiful U-shaped pink velvet sectional seats a bunch of people who are drinking cocktails, eating gourmet finger foods, and engaging in lively conversations. The guests seem to know each other, which makes me feel even more uncomfortable. I don't fit in, and I'm not the sort of person who works very hard at it. Either my friends and I are a good fit or we aren't. I guess tonight I'll find out if the twins and I are meant to be friends.

Folding my arms timidly, I search the faces for a glimpse of one twin or the other. So far, nobody is recognizable except... I lock eyes with Lynx Grove, who's standing in front of three tall slash windows that display views of a garden lit by fairy lights. Another athletically built man stands with him as well as three stylish women.

I raise a hand and wave at him. Lynx waves back. He says something to the group. Before I can go to him, he's coming to me. The tension that had been trapped inside me ever since I left my apartment is slowly leaving me. Lynx Grove feels so familiar for so many reasons. I'm not sure I can be friends with Orion, but I can definitely see myself being friends with Lynx.

"Hey you," he says as I go in for the hug.

"Fancy seeing you here," I say.

We're saying a lot as we look downward to chuckle. The coincidence that we ended up at this party alone is remarkable.

"I'm surprised I didn't run into you in the elevator, Mr. Eleventh Floor."

I'm flirty and the sparkle in his eyes reveals that he likes it.

Lynx's hand is on my arm. His touch is warm, strong, soft, but calloused. "You want a drink?"

I pause. It kind of would be nice to lose my head with this particular guy. However, if Lynx stands me up against a wall and bangs my brains out, I want to remember it. "Only the nonalcoholic kind," I reply.

On that note he went off to fetch me a tonic water with fresh lime. He's drinking brandy because it relaxes him. He says even though he's at a party, he can use some relaxation. Work has been hard this week. We've carved ourselves two comfortable seats on the big pink sofa. Lynx has revealed that he missed the opportunity to start something with his friend.

"She was single only for a hot minute. I guess, I snoozed and lost." He snorts, simpering. I can see that he's really feeling the loss of this lucky woman.

"But does she know you're interested?" I ask.

He sighs as he sinks more into the sofa, and crosses his legs at the ankle as they stretch across a round black leather ottoman. "Yeah. I think so."

I sink against the sofa too and stretch my legs close to his. I feel no sparks. I think it's the fact that he's in love with another woman. I hope so. I hope it's not because I have feelings for Orion. I plead with my heart to please don't let that be the case.

I let my head drop to one side so that I can get a better look at him. "You think so?"

"Yeah, I think so."

"Have you ever told her how you felt?"

He nervously loosens a button on his black silk shirt that his hilly chest is wearing the hell out of. "Yeah, sort of."

"Sort of? Are you afraid to clearly articulate how you feel about her?"

"Huh?" he asks, frowning and confused. "No. I just want her to be happy."

I grunt thoughtfully. Lynx is such a good guy, but he's like every other man like him. He's a city boy through and through. City boys spend all their lives striving for success in their careers. Love scares the hell out of them. My guess is that he's tethered to this woman, but he's afraid of what she inspires in him and therefore hasn't made a deliberate move to claim her.

"She's dating someone else, you say?"

"Yeah," he croaks and then sighs.

"What if this other guy steps up to the plate and hits a home run?"

His chuckle is smooth like silk. The brandy must be working. He's good and relaxed. "Then we're not meant to be, Lilly. What about you?"

I sit up so that I can better drink my beverage. "What about me?"

"What's going on between you and Orion?"

My eyebrows flash up. Why is *he* asking me that question?

"You seem surprised," he says, scanning my face.

"I'm surprise you're asking me that."

Lynx shrugs indifferently. "He likes you. Maybe he's waiting for me to swing a home run before he does something about it."

I inhale sharply, surprised by what he just said. There is pure lust in Lynx's eyes. That's when I remember how easily my looks fell into place tonight. I left my apartment looking like sex on a stick. Maybe, just maybe, I'll drop my guard for this one. Maybe, just maybe, tonight is cosmic. Fate is working on our behalf. Maybe this is the moment all the incidences with Orion have been building up to.

I feel dizzy even though I'm not drunk when I say, "Maybe. Definitely, maybe."

CHAPTER 17
Rescue His Heart

ORION LORD

FORTY-THREE MINUTES AGO

My mother has been summoning me to her town house here on the Upper East Side a lot lately. Every time I show up, Heather is here. I know what my mom is doing and it's not going to work. I can't tell her that though, can I? Since working with Lila on AI behavior mapping, I learned a lot about human psychology. For instance, on Thursday, as we worked through lunch, Delilah explained the mother/son dynamic in a way that made me clearly understand it for the first time. We were discussing indigenous human behavior and the benefits of mapping AI behavior to those traits.

She explained how boys left the cocoon fashioned by their mothers at or around the age of fourteen in indigenous tribes from one part of the world to the next.

"There's something to it, don't you think?" she asked.

"What do you mean?" I asked, stroking my chin. I wanted to know more about this.

"Young males go learn to hunt and survive, and the older men of the tribe, who had gone through the same initiation rites, teach them how to be men. In some cases, boys are ripped away from their mothers crying. She's reaching for him. He's reaching for her. But the tribe knows that for his sanity, for his development, it must be done."

I'm not sure if she meant to affect me with that explanation or not, but she had. Tonight, as I sit at the table having dinner with my mother, Heather, and Peter, my mother's partner, who's twenty years younger than she is, I'm uncomfortable. I feel like I'm in a vise, unable to move left or right, or escape. I think it's always been this way with my mother.

"Well, I think Orion and I can head up the Labor Day Gala together. He has a powerful contacts list and so do I." Grinning, Heather winks at me. "We're good together."

"Well, I concur," my mother says, rubbing her palms together happily.

It's as if I'm having an out-of-body experience. I can't let this farce to continue, but I've always allowed it and played my role well. Lila also said that love is like blood. I've come to the conclusion that my mother's love has been too much like blood. It's time to cut the feeding tube and create a different dynamic, a healthier one.

My cell phone, which is in my pants pocket, buzzes just as I'm about to address the exchange that has taken place between Heather and my mother. My phone performed jumpy buzzing instead of a smooth consistent buzzing, and that alerts me that the caller is part of my close contact list.

"Hello," I say, after sliding my cell phone out of my pocket.

"Oh, come on," Heather grouses.

"That's not good manners," Marigold adds.

"Hey, O, guess who's at my party?"

I'm on my feet and striding out of the dining room. "Mina—I forgot about your party."

"Thanks a lot. But Lilly hasn't forgot about my party though."

I stop in the middle of the hallway and turn to

face a mirror that's attached to the wall. "Delilah?" I ask.

I ARRIVE AT MINA'S PLACE. I ALMOST DIDN'T GO back into the dining room. I could've walked out without facing the wrath of Heather and my mother. But avoidance meant I wasn't ready to deal with the issue of my mother head-on. I went back into the kitchen and excused myself.

"What?" Heather gasped. "You can't leave. Who does that?"

Looking at the seconds tick by on my watch, I said, "Being that I thought I was coming over here to look over documents for my mother and got roped into a dinner I didn't plan for, I figure I can leave. Good night, Heather."

Heather leaped to her feet. "Well, I'm going with you."

"You're not invited." I kiss my mother on the forehead. "We'll have a discussion later," I said to her.

"Are you sure you can't stay? The cook made your favorite," Marigold said.

I took a moment to acknowledge the look on my

mother's face. Right then and there I realized that it was me who was hanging on. My mother had no real stake in whether I came or went. She merely loves and likes my company. Heather has been taking advantage of that fact.

"I can't stay, Mother." I kissed her on top of the head. I froze, suddenly experiencing déjà vu. But the person I kissed this way wasn't my mother. It was Delilah. I want her. I fucking want her. And I'd better get to Mina's party quickly. The last thing Mina revealed to me was that Delilah had gotten chummy with Lynx Grove. There's no way I'm going to another Grove wedding where somebody I love, truly love, is getting married to someone else.

I headed down the hallway with Heather screaming after me, "Wait, Orion! You can't leave without me!"

She wrapped me up from behind and held me. I thought, *This woman's fucking crazy. I should've ended it with her a long time ago.* When I made Lila break dates last winter, I had decided to work on my relationships with women. The wake-up calls for me were Herc capturing me on video getting a blow job by someone he was being forced to marry. The other punch in the gut that made me question the way I dealt with women was Treasure choosing Achilles. I thought for sure she would choose me first or eventually choose me later.

On February 14, Valentine's Day, I had run into Treasure at Mother's town house. It was the first time since she'd been with Achilles that we were able to talk alone. And so I asked her, "Why not me? Why him?"

"Because I love him," she had said.

"But not at first," I quickly countered.

"That's easy," she said, making sure I couldn't look away from her eyes. "You are incapable of love. I mean really, Orion, do you love me? Unconditionally, and want to spend the rest of your life with me?"

I immediately considered her question and became spooked as one person came to mind. Someone I couldn't shake. The reason why I called Delilah on the weekends, bothered her to no end, was because I always wanted more of her.

"No," I had said. "I can't see myself with you forever."

"I know," she had said and then strolled back down the hallway to help my mother choose Lake Clark artwork for the new townhome.

There was no need to confess that she was right about me being unable to truly love one woman.

Being someone's all in all, or other half, and then relying on her to be the same for me scared the hell out of me. But Delilah has been my other half for four and a half years. However, I've been shit to her. I want to turn that around. That's what I was thinking when Heather tightened her grip on me and whimpered, "Please don't go."

"Heather," my mother called, her voice stern and assertive. "Let go of my son—now."

I could feel Heather's grip loosen as she kept repeating, "Please."

"Sorry," I whispered once she had completely let go of me. I kept walking until the reeking and humid night air of late June plugged my nostrils. Then I took a deeper breath. There was not much I found more invigorating than the trashy, dirty, stinking air of New York City. I was on my way to get my girl.

As soon as I walk inside Lina meets me at the door.

"Fuck, what took you so long?" She shakes her head. "Never mind. I'll worry about him. And you get her."

"Is that why Mina called me?" I ask following Lina. "Lila is cockblocking you?"

Lina turns but doesn't look at me or slow her pace. "Yes, indeed."

Then I see her. Her black dress is so high up her thigh that I can almost glimpse my favorite place. She looks absolutely stunning tonight. I want her. Like gravity, her eyes lock on mine. My chest tightens as my smile wavers. Is she happy to see me? I can't tell. She and Lynx stand up as if they are about to leave together, making me wonder if I'm too late.

CHAPTER 18

A Change of Heart and Heat

DELILAH O'SHAY

The strangest thing just happened. Lina, arms wide open to embrace me and wearing a red bandage dress, sashayed over and in a singsong voice said, "Lilly, so glad you can make it. Do you mind if I steal Lynx for a moment?" She kissed near one of my cheeks and then the other.

Lynx and I raised our eyebrows at each other. Something had just happened between us before Lina and Orion arrived.

We were still sitting on the sofa when he had asked, "You would go out with me?" He sounded as if it would surprise him if I said yes.

"Who wouldn't?" I said.

"But I work a lot," he offered up.

I tilted my head from one side to the other. "So do I."

"My family's mad," he said with a laugh.

"So is mine."

"Sorry, Lilly…" He clicked his teeth and winked. "I got you beat there."

"How so?"

"Whenever my family gets together my mother and my aunt fight like Godzilla and King Kong." He curled his fingers and pushed one hand at the other, and then back and forth to orchestrate how they fight. "You're sitting at the dinner table with these people and then wham, you're in the middle of a *Pinky and the Brain* world takeover plan orchestrated by my father and my uncle like the shit they cooked up with the Lords."

I jerked my head back. "What shit did they cook up with the Lords?"

"Can't tell you," he said as if he didn't at all regret letting that little revelation slip. I thought he was done until he raised a finger almost in slow motion and said, "Also my father will pile it on by making slick remarks about how disappointed he is that I'm in professional sports instead of tech."

"But you own the baseball team. That's a huge deal."

"Not to him."

"Wow," I mouthed, and then quickly shifted in my seat, allowing the front of my body to face him as a question came to mind. "So, Lynx, are you telling me this to dissuade me from liking you?"

Wearing a crooked smile, one of Lynx's eyebrows shot up. "You like me?"

I snorted, chuckling. "I think that's been established."

We stared into each other's eyes, letting my declaration sink in. The longer we sat there that way, the more something inside me clicked, and then locked, and then the key was given to someone else.

My smile and my soul felt full of resolve. "But maybe we have more of a friend connection."

"I agree," he said without pause and then asked, "By the way, are you hungry?" He rubbed his fabulous six-pack, which was perceptible through the shirt he's wearing. "Because I'm starving."

I told him I was too and then we got up to find the servers who were carrying the shrimp tempura, and that's when I saw Orion. A wave of giddy energy rippled through me. I'm hit by another wave of that delicious energy as Orion's gaze spreads through me and saturates my heart with his desire.

"You look really beautiful tonight."

I lap him up with my own intense look. "So do you."

He chuckles a little.

"O!" a guy calls.

We rip our gazes off each other. It's Ben and he's with two guys who look familiar.

His buddies are getting close, but Orion takes me by the hand and guides me in the opposite direction.

"Oh, it's like that, O," one of the guys says.

"Hello, Delilah," Ben croons. I recognize his voice.

Every person we pass pays us special attention. Some say hello to Orion, and he doesn't say it back. He's focused on where he's taking me. I can't believe I'm letting him. All of my vital organs feel like they're throbbing and my blood has warmed. I want to melt with Orion Lord and it behooves me to resolve this craving before I lose all self-restraint.

We make it to the grand foyer. Earlier I was too nervous to notice the chevron marble flooring, ceiling coffers, and a beautifully ornate chandelier. The design principle is so vintage but also modern. It's odd that I'm noticing that while in such a heightened emotional state. I think it's because the atmosphere is so rich, so alien. Suddenly, I get a flash of perspective. We've made it to the porch and by the way he's looking at me, it's clear what he wants. No matter what Orion says or does, no matter how much I crave him, there will be no sex with the notorious fuckboy.

"HOW ABOUT WE GO BACK TO MY PLACE?" ORION asks, hands in his pockets as we stand on the porch. He's leaning into me and I just might lose all my willpower.

I look away from his eyes and connect with tonight's big beautiful full moon.

"Wow," I say. "What a night."

I glance to see that his eyes have followed mine. "It's beautiful, like you." But now he's watching me again and with arousing intensity. "Were you about to go home with Lynx?"

I stiffen, caught off guard by his question. "No."

Orion studies me as if he's searching for truth. "Are you coming home with me?"

I'm sensitive to so much as the answer to his question sits on my tongue. I let my chest rise high with each breath reviving me as my pulse races around that moon we've just admired. My body craves making love to Orion tonight. But…

"No," I whisper.

He steps closer, and draws me against him. "Are you certain?"

The hardness of his body is about to sink this determined ship. But I'm standing at a fork in the road. It's incumbent upon me to make the right decision.

"Do you like me, Orion?" I whisper and then swallow. I watch him intently, feeling like the state of my heart depends on the answer to his question.

"Very much, Lila—very much."

Ooh…the bliss I'm experiencing is like the best drug. "Then date me."

When he smirks, a flash of his white teeth makes his mouth look so mouthwatering. I want to kiss him feverishly.

"Date you?"

"Umm-hmm," I say, my head feeling buoyant as I nod. "Date me."

"That should be fun," he says to my surprise.

"I think so."

His lips have moved closer. "But can I kiss you first?"

I nod.

Not a second passes before Orion's mouth has swept mine up and against his. My body feels like the consistency of jelly as he holds me tightly. My fingers entertain the back of his head. One of his hands slips up my thigh, squeezes my ass, and draws me against his magnificent boner. It's mind-boggling to know that Orion Lord wants me that much.

"You're so fucking soft," he whispers thickly. "But…" His lips abandon mine. His hands release my body. I'm standing here, aching for him, shivering with need. "We're dating, not fucking."

CHAPTER 19
The Billionaire and Me
DELILAH O'SHAY

I t has been two and a half weeks since we revised the nature of our deal. Initially I was to see less of Orion over the weekends but now I'm spending more time with him than ever, to Xena's disappointment.

"He's going to end up hurting you," she said once, and then promised she'll never say it again. Then my cousin took me by the face. "But never fear, I love you unconditionally. I'll be here to help you pick up the pieces of your heart that he's going to shatter and spread over the Hudson where all the other bodies are buried."

"Eek," I said, frowning.

"Yeah...eek," my cousin replied.

So far, Orion has shown no signs that he's even

close to obliterating my heart. At the office, we mostly work on the AI software. When he's close to me, my skin feels tickles of lust, especially when he leans over my shoulder to look at the computer screen. He knows what his nearness does to me and, knowing him, he gets a charge out of making me horny. Orion is waiting for me to break. But I won't break. I like our dates too much. I'm afraid of what will happen to us if I start changing the nature of our relationship. But I don't think I can resist him for long. Also, the fact that I've been keeping the matter of waking up wearing a ring after our wild night out together is still vexing me. I should just tell him. I don't know what's keeping me from doing it.

"Hey!" Orion says as he bolts into the office.

He's been out all morning in his secret basement lab.

Hand on my heart, I'm settling down from being startled. "Hi."

"I'm sorry for startling you, but we have to get going."

"Get going?"

Orion quirks an eyebrow and smirks slightly. "I've been taking every date up a notch, haven't I?"

He *has* taken every date up a notch. On the night we decided to start this adventure, his driver took us to his penthouse apartment on Billionaires' Row. It was the first time I've ever stepped foot in such a posh living space. Everything was fresh and new. The white ultra-modern decor blew my mind. His place is definitely an extreme bachelor's pad. I recall thinking that he lived like a man who has no intentions on ever getting married. But Orion had made me filet mignon with mashed potatoes that he peeled, baked, and smashed himself. For dessert we shared a small carton of vanilla ice cream. We talked until the sun came up. I learned more about his relationship with his father. Once a year he takes a trip to spend a week with Christopher Lord. He said his parents divorced at the end of twenty-five years. His parents are distant cousins who married each other to benefit from the Lord family trust. They liked each other, but never loved each other. His father, Chris, wants nothing to do with the money and being forced to marry Marigold has scarred him for life.

I couldn't believe he shared that with me. I wish I had something on a similar scale to share with him, but I didn't. The more Orion confessed his regrets and fears, the more normal my existence and family felt.

"That's why the love of money is indeed the root to all evil," he had said.

"The love of it," I replied.

"Yes. To love it."

We kissed until we were on his floor, rolling around on top of a white faux fur rug. It would've been so easy to go all the way. Even after he touched me, got me off, and made me so wet and ready for him, Orion did not cross the line.

We've gone to see three Broadway shows. He even introduced me to Lonnie Blaine, the most successful Broadway producer alive. He's won twenty-one Tony awards in various categories. The man is a star and he also makes stars.

"She's a great dancer," Orion said.

I could tell that Blaine didn't quite take him seriously until Orion revealed that I had to quit my dreams of performing for someone like him to take care of my father. He's been a demanding boss. I saved his hide on several occasions. If it weren't for me, he wouldn't know what to do. After hearing all of that, Lonnie became more interested in me as a person and a performer. He gave me his card and told me to call his number and his assistant will add me to the auditions mailing list.

I'm on the mailing list. That date was definitely epic.

We've spent a weekend sailing on his yacht, catching rays, eating my favorite biscuits, swimming, dancing, and getting close to sex but stopping ourselves before he "inserts penis here." But he would search my eyes. Orion wanted me to make the move. And when I didn't, he simply put more physical distance between us.

Also, for the past two weeks, we've eaten dinner together every night at all the top restaurants in the city, including Treasure's.

"How did the two of you come to be?" I had asked.

In Treasure's restaurant, while eating some of the best food I ever tasted, he explained how they met.

"She came to me and threatened me to leave her brother alone."

I gasped in shock. "Lynx?"

"Yeah. We went to the same high school."

"You bullied Lynx?" That was news to me since the two of them seemed to get along well enough.

"Not me. I'm a lover, not a bully." He winked at me and I laughed. "Others bullied him on my behalf."

He didn't go into much detail, which I appreciated. I could see that heading back down memory lane and entertaining thoughts of his brother's wife made him uncomfortable.

"We were young, and didn't know much about having something real beyond fucking. Like this, with us," he had said. "This feels real."

That was two days ago, and the highlight of my life. I want to make love to him now. I was going to seduce him after dinner. But he's still waiting to hear my answer. Has he taken every date up a notch?

"Yes, and then some," I say, grinning from ear to ear.

"Come here," he whispers with a lift of his chin as if commanding me.

It works because I'm on my feet and now our bodies are flattened against each other. I will never stop being turned on by his hardness. It's as if he's made of granite.

"Let's get the fuck out of here," he says and then kisses me deeply.

HEADS AGAINST THE BACK SEAT, AND FACING EACH other, Orion and I made out all the way to the airport. It occurs to me when we board his private jet after walking up the ramp with woozy legs why we've been able to narrowly avoid sex for two weeks. Our kissing is almost just as gratifying as the act itself—almost. There's nothing like a real orgasm, and Orion has rubbed me to orgasm several times to remind me what I'm missing.

We have one male flight attendant named Jason. Orion and I haven't taken our seats yet. We're positioned in the middle of a circular platform built in the center of the cabin. My body is still feverish from making out with him. I'm wearing a stiff sheet dress with a boatneck collar that made it difficult for his hands to directly stimulate my most sensitive parts while kissing. But my panties are drenched, my nipples are at attention from his pinching, and my cells are reaching out to him.

"The bedroom," he says, eyebrows up.

"Yes. The bedroom."

WE BANG AGAINST ONE WALL, TONGUING DEEP. Orion has my dress by the hem and for a moment my mouth releases his as inflexible black material shoots up over my head, leaving me in my heels, bra, and panties.

"Oh," Orion murmurs softly as he takes a step back and pinches his chin, admiring my body. He's getting several eyefuls of me. "You have the sexiest body, baby."

He doesn't retreat back into me as I twist my torso in pure unadulterated lust. I needed his hands on me a second ago. Instead, Orion steps out of his expensive trousers. My breaths grow deeper and faster at the sight of his cock pushing against his flawless black underwear. He unbuttons and takes off his shirt. The hills and crooks of his chest and abs make me want to lose it.

"Wow," I sigh.

"Wow indeed," Orion replies as he steps close again and pinches the waistband of my panties. Our exhales crash as I gaze dizzily into his eyes.

"Prepare for takeoff," the captain's voice projects through the intercom.

I'm the first to break the control of our lustful haze with a laugh.

"Are we supposed to go back out there and strap ourselves in?" I ask.

Orion's lips show no hint of a smile as he

unclips the latch at the front of my bra, freeing my breasts.

He involuntarily releases a sigh and then my head falls back as the warmth and wetness of his mouth gobbles up my right breast and then my left, licking, sucking, nibbling. I suck air, my palms pressing against the fiberglass wall as Orion tastes down my sternum, my belly, and then his tongue presses into my belly button over and over again while he finishes taking off my panties.

I can feel the airplane still taxiing as Orion's tongue sinks over my clit.

I moan tightly as that divine sensation of stimulation instantly makes my legs grow weaker.

"Relax, baby," Orion whispers. He must certainly feel the tension in my thighs and pussy. I'm a stickler for the rules, and he is not.

But he's licking me again, and his large hands have my thighs in a vise grip. I'm not going anywhere but staying right here, against the wall.

"Oh," I say in a shiver as I hold on to the back of his head. "Oh…" That came out in a loud high-pitched voice because an orgasm is popping off in my sex like firecrackers.

I'm still reeling from the pleasure when Orion is suddenly on his feet. While dizzy and weak in the legs, I watch his arm stretch above my head. Two handrails automatically move outward on both sides of our bodies.

"Hold on, baby," he whispers as he loops my arms around the metal links. He grabs hold too and as the airplane zooms down the runway, I taste myself in Orion's mouth.

S-E-X

"I'm going to come," I squeal in a tense voice.

I'm on top of him. He has two handfuls of me as he shifts me expertly against his cock. My sex quivers as it tightens against him and then, halting all breathing, my mouth is caught open as I try to scream at the top of my lungs.

Now it's his turn.

The master of sex that he is, my sexy man rotates me onto my back in one smooth fell swoop. His strong body is between my thighs. I can't take my eyes off his face as I hazily watch what he looks like as he strokes my pussy. I'm in love with this man, I admit. That acknowledgment doesn't even scare me anymore. But does he love me?

He says "umm" after his final thrust and then his whole-body shivers and he whimpers, letting loose inside me. I don't care. I would have this man's babies. *I would so have his babies.*

NIGHT OUT

Orion had come so hard that he didn't get it up again until after we landed in New Orleans. So, we made love on the runway. Now we're dancing in a small club on Frenchman Street. Orion knows all the musicians, bouncers, and bartenders. He says he visits the city often. It's one of his favorite places in the world. Next week he's going to take me to his second favorite place, which is Paris, France. A friend of his, a French rapper named Alex Dupont, is giving us front row seats to his concert.

We go to Antoine's Restaurant for dinner. Instead of sitting across the table from me, Orion puts his chair right next to mine.

"Now, are we still only dating? Or are we more?" he asks.

His face so close to mine, I kiss him softly. It's

such a sensually soft kiss that I do it again, and then say breathlessly. "We're more."

"Orion?" a curious female's voice says.

We both rip our attention off each other to see the woman who's all legs and exceptionally gorgeous face standing at the edge of our table. *I've seen her before.* Not in real life though.

Orion quickly removes his arm from the back of my chair. "Gabrielle?"

Gabrielle, the ending pronouncement of her name is "ay," Gabriell-e, is probably the most beautiful woman in the world. Her dark eyes can set any man's loins on fire and her body, wrapped in a pink silk dress that fits her like a glove, is even making me feverish. Her mere presence reminds me what I've forgotten—I'm not stunning enough for Orion Lord. I can already feel his desire for me dwindle and flow to her.

"I didn't know you were going to be in town," she says. Finally, she looks at me as if she's seeing me for the first time. Her eyes widen just a bit. Funny, she almost appears as sad as I feel.

"This is…" Orion presses his lips unsure of how to refer to me even though we've just made declarations of being together with each other.

I'm about to help him remember my name

when he flashes that toothy smile that I've come to crave and says, "This is my new girlfriend, Lilly."

Then, he turns and gazes at me as if she's chopped liver and I'm the most beautiful woman in the room.

IT'S AFTER MIDNIGHT WHEN WE'RE ON THE AIRPLANE flying back to New York City. We've just banged out all the sexual tension tonight had built in us. Regardless, I still can't get Gabrielle out of my head. After Orion introduced me as his girlfriend, Gabrielle said, "Oh, nice, um, I should be getting back to my friends. Have a fun trip."

"Thanks, I will," he said and didn't give her a second glance as she went back to wherever she came from.

Even though Orion clearly chose me, my insecurity won't let me truly believe it. As I lay my head on his bare chest, I can hear his heart thumping. He's at ease lying here with my face on his skin. I think I should ask him about her now.

"Gabrielle," I say and listen harder for any changes in his heartbeats. There's no change.

"What about her?" he says.

"You used to have a relationship with her?"

He chuckles and the sound creates a deep vibration against my ear.

"What's so funny?" I ask, smiling pensively.

"You didn't ask if she was my girlfriend because you know I don't do girlfriends." I close my eyes and smile when he kisses the top of my head. "And so does she."

"But you called me your girlfriend," I say.

"Because you are Lilly...Lila..." Orion pauses. "I like Lila, still."

I chuckle. "Then Lila it is."

Orion flips me onto my back, and says, "Guess what?" now that he's between my thighs.

I can already feel it as he moves into me and I gasp with pleasure.

CHAPTER 20

Breaking The News

ORION LORD

Umm...*shit.*

A kiss is never simply a kiss with Lila. I search over my shoulder, counting the steps between her desk to the top of mine. I fucked her on my desk on Friday of last week, the morning after our New Orleans trip, and then again on Monday and Tuesday. What can I say, I like doing her on my desk. It's pent-up frustration from all those days of looking at her sitting across from me and me thinking, *I'd like to fuck her right now.* Today is Wednesday. Last night was the first full night we hadn't slept together. I was in the lab for twenty-four hours perfecting my AI software. Today, I'm presenting it to Herc. It was like pulling teeth getting my brother to take a look at what I came up with. I know it will be an uphill battle once I'm alone with him. It would be nice to go upstairs sexually satisfied.

"Orion, not now," Lila says, following my eyes to my desk.

"Come on, babe. A quickie." She's so fucking tight. My cock is always happy at first thrust when I move inside her. "It won't take me a minute."

Her soft hands wrap around my wrist. She lifts my arm so I can see my watch. "Orion, you have less than five minutes the last I checked. You don't want to be late for this meeting. Remember, we talked through this already."

I sigh long and hard. Lila and I had indeed talked it through. I love that I can trust her enough to reveal that I'm battling an urge to drop the ball and keep with business as usual. I fuck up and Herc walks away proud of himself for having me pegged. But I've been doing a hell of a lot differently recently, including being loyal to one woman. When Lila and I ran into Gabrielle last week, that weak feeling that one look at her used to put in my stomach wasn't there. She's an undeniable beauty but so is Lila. The only difference is Lila doesn't need the whole world to worship her for her looks. Watching the two of them in one room put it all into perspective for me. I prefer Lila's style of being. I find her sexier and more trustworthy. I'm ready to make her Mrs. Orion Lord today. But I know her— she'll need our relationship to work for at least a year before saying yes to marrying me.

"All right," I say, begrudgingly accepting defeat. "Shit. What am I going to do with this hard-on?" I readjust my cock in my pants.

She moans seductively and kisses me quickly on the cheek. "We could pick up where we're leaving when you get back."

"Deal," I say as I take her by the waist and tug her against me.

My lips are on hers and our soft kiss me light-headed. But when she slaps my ass, I come back to myself.

"Now go get it done, Mr. Orion Lord," she says with two hands on my chest, playfully shoving me away from her.

"When I get back…" I point to my desk. "Be ready." I wink at her.

Gracing me with her beautiful grin, she salutes me. "Aye, aye, boss."

I get an easy smile just thinking about the treat that comes at the end of this fucking presentation. I almost forgot that nobody can ice my hard-on faster than my brother. I only hope I can get it up soon after I'm done dealing with him.

"Oh, Orion," Lila calls before I'm out of sight.

I turn back. My heart melts at the sight of her gleaming at me with her thumb up.

"Good luck, babe," she says.

I wink at her. "Thank you."

HERC HAS A HUGE CORNER OFFICE. IT LOOKS JUST as important as he likes to make himself feel. I'll hand it to my brother, he's a smart guy. I like him. I've noticed he and Lila have a lot in common. They are both experts in excelling while following the rules. They're two people who know how to keep a clear conscience.

I walk into his office and he quickly says to whoever he's talking to on the phone, "I have a meeting. We'll continue this later."

He ends his call, and then he's up, and we're hugging. I feel the love emanating from me and him. We love each other, and that can't be rebutted. But respect? Now that's a whole other ball game.

"I want to talk to you, Orion," Herc says on the

way back to his chair as if he's the one who arranged our meeting.

"Did you view the package I sent you before-hand?" I ask.

"You mean the AI shit?" He shakes his head. "We're not currently interested in AI, you know this."

Here we go. "But you'll get interested in AI when you see our product—"

"Have you spoken to Achilles?" he asks, cutting me off.

I go motionless, staring at his face. He's not taking me seriously at all. What does he want? Does he want me to rot on the first floor, crunching unnecessary numbers?

"Herc, I want you to take me seriously. I can head up an AI division. I've seen the numbers—we can afford this."

My brother runs a finger through his hair as he mocks me with a laugh. "You want me to take you seriously when you can't stop being a fucking liability?"

I frown, confused as hell.

"Have you spoken to Achilles?" he asks again. There's an edge in his tone and also in the way he's sitting there smug and judgmental.

"What do you mean by me being a fucking liability?"

His face gets pinched the way it does when he's ready to stop imploding and explode. "We put a lot of work into carving out a deal with the Groves to get around those fucking purity clauses. And from where I sit, all you're good for is blowing up shit. If me marrying Lauren had been our last resort, you blew that shit up. You tried to blow up Achilles and Treasure, which was part of the deal. Do you know you're married, Orion? We can't risk an annulment because…"

I jerk my head back. "What?"

"Of course, you don't know."

He goes on to tell me that the maid found a diamond ring in the bathroom's trash can in the suite I stayed in while in Las Vegas. The ring had a serial number inside the band. Achilles had it tracked to a chapel that sold me the ring in care of Delilah O'Shay. Then, he sent me a video of my wedding ceremony and suggested I watch it privately.

"It gets kind of rated R at the end."

A ring in the bathroom's trash can? Did Lila toss the ring and never told me about it? I'm pissed. It takes everything in me to keep it together. I have to compartmentalize or I'll blow any potential deal with Herc.

My mouth is so tight, my jaw aches, and I don't know if I'm coming or going. "What about my AI software?"

Herc looks cold as he pulls the corners of his mouth down and says, "Not interested."

I've seen that look on his face before. He's too angry at me. *Fuck.* "You know this is good."

Herc falls back in his chair and swivels. "Yeah, it's good. How about you sell it to me?"

"What do you mean by, 'sell it to you'?"

"I'll pay for the research and your team. Or did you use my employees?"

I snort bitterly. "No, and no."

"It's your track record, Orion. But if you really want to contribute to this business for real, I can put you back in sales."

I narrow my eyes, taking in my bother's face. Look at him... He's waiting for my woe-is-me reply. He's expecting me to say how unfair he's being and that he wants to keep me down to make himself look good. The truth is, Herc has shouldered a lot of our family problems. He's the one who figured out how to keep LTI afloat. He came up with a solution to not only have our branch of the Lord family take over the family trust but bring a halt to the distasteful practice of intermarrying for a financial benefit.

I sit up straight and take this shit like a man. "Okay. I fucked up. We'll get the marriage annulled..."

"You know you can't do that. An annulment to an outsider puts the trust in jeopardy. You married her without a prenup." He throws his hands up and drops them hard on his desk. "Achilles will reach out to Delilah to make a deal with her. Yet again, he's cleaning up your fuckup."

I'm all out of words. I stand and turn my back on my brother. I can't feel my legs as I walk out of his office.

"How about business development," Herc says when I reach the door. "I could put you there and you can use that expensive ivy league degree of yours for real this time."

Fuck him. I don't say anything to him as I walk out of his office, closing the door hard behind me.

BEFORE I ENTER THE ELEVATOR, I WATCH THE VIDEO Herc sent me. "Shit!" *We fucked in the chapel?*

I storm into the elevator and smash the first-floor button so hard my finger almost goes through it. I shake my head continuously. How will Lila answer for this? I thought I could trust her, but apparently not.

CHAPTER 21
Fallout

DELILAH O'SHAY

I hop to my feet as soon as Orion sweeps into the office. "How did it go?"

"Guess what?" he asks.

I've never seen him look so austere. "What?" I barely say. I'm worried about what happened between him and Hercules.

"The maid found a diamond ring in my trash can. I bought it when we got married while we were fucking hammered. Do you want to see our wedding? We end with a bang, literally."

My eyes keep expanding as my head feels like it's floating to a galaxy far, far away.

"Do you know how a ring I bought for you ended up in the trash can, Lila?"

Tears burn the backs of my eyes as I nod. I have to tell the truth now.

Orion looks so disappointed in me. I can't stop my tears from rolling.

"Were you ever going to tell me?"

I nod again.

"When?"

"I don't know," I barely say.

He snatches his glower off me and stares at the wall.

"I'm sorry," I say in a tiny and ineffectual voice. "You have no idea how sorry I am."

I search his face, looking for any sign of sympathy, empathy, or forgiveness. But all I see is anger, hurt, and sadness. He doesn't give me a second glance as he walks to the door and puts his hand on the knob. "I'll text you our wedding video. And, um, you can leave for the day."

I'm speechless. I have no defense for not telling him other than I was horrified to wake up in his bed that morning. To me, he was still Boss Scoundrel. But he hasn't been that in quite a while. I could have told him. I should have told him. The truth is, I was afraid that I had waited too long.

"And, um, your two weeks' notice? Accepted.

You don't have to come back. I'll pay for the month."

"Orion?" I chirp like a hurt bird.

But so quickly the door is opened and he's gone.

As I walk home, I feel like I'm moving in an alternate universe. The New York afternoon is particularly alive today. The heat is sweltering. The bars and cafés are packed. Everyone's out already enjoying the period before the cold is ushered in. I, on the other hand, already feel the winter. I can't stop shivering, and my tears won't stop rolling either. I don't care who sees me.

Eventually, I make it back to my apartment. I drag myself into my bedroom, fall on my bed, lie on my back, and stare at the ceiling. I'm aware that time is passing, but I can't look away from this little speck of black in the white paint above my bed. I perceive the light is changing all around me. My cell phone beeps in my purse, letting me know I received a message.

Why didn't I tell him? I could've said, "Oh, Orion, one more thing...." And then just said it. He probably would've laughed his ass off at our calamitous drunken behavior. I'm sure Hercules rubbed his nose in his mistake. Orion must've been embarrassed to find out that way, especially when I already knew. You don't have to be a rocket scientist to find out that I'm the one who tossed the ring in the trash. His brothers know. Their wives know. I humiliated him and he'll never forgive me.

I sniff and wipe the swiftly moving tears off the side of my face. Then I curl up on my side. My phone rings and announces that the caller is Xena. I practically leap off the bed to answer her call. It's time I tell her the truth too.

TWO HOURS LATER

Xena's back in my bedroom with a box of tissues and a wet facecloth to wipe my face.

"Never cry over a boy, Delilah," she says for the second time.

"He's not a boy," I whine. "Orion is all man."

She rolls her eyes. I told her everything. I'm clearly the one in the wrong. But she still hates him so he's probably always going to be the one who's wrong in her eyes.

Xena sighs. "Okay, Lilly, I get that you fell in love with him, and it sounds like he fell in love with you. I'm saying not to cry because if he's the kind of guy who can break it off with you because you didn't tell him about the most embarrassing moment of your life, and his life too, then fuck him. You deserve better."

I'm sure she's making a great point but at the moment my emotions won't let me absorb what she's saying.

"Have you eaten dinner?" she asks, rubbing my ankle soothingly.

I shake my head. "But I can't go out."

"I'll cook something for us. You have food in the fridge, don't you?"

I nod. Of course, I have food in the fridge. "Do you want to see the video?"

Xena throws both her hands up. "No, I do not." She shakes her finger at me. "I don't want you berating yourself about this anymore either. You screwed up. Move on because life moves on. The world continues to evolve. And yesterday is no longer in existence. That's what Herald would say to you, right?"

Herald's my dad.

"Yes."

Still pointing at me, she says, "Don't forget it. And listen, I'm taking my own advice. Because the world is fucked."

One face comes to mind. "David?"

"He and I are officially over. For good this time."

I don't believe her at all. I've never known a couple to be on and off so much.

"So," she says and springs to her feet. "No more wallowing in self-pity. If Uncle Herald had wallowed in self-pity, he wouldn't be running today." And on that note, she strolls out of my bedroom and on her way to the kitchen to make us something to eat.

When I'm alone again, I flop back down on my bed. I knew it was wise to take her call. She's right. I screwed up. And Orion has a right to be mad at me. I'll give him time to cool off. We have to talk at some point in time because we're married. *OMG, we're married!* But for now, I'll take Xena's advice and try to live in the moment. I find that last grain of oomph sparking inside and get to my feet. After a few deep breaths, I head into the kitchen to help Xena find something to cook.

4 DAYS LATER

Three days ago, Achilles called me and offered me ten million dollars to remain married to Orion. It took all my strength to keep myself from breaking down over the phone.

"Absolutely not," I had mustered up enough composure to say. I agreed to stay married to Orion for as long as the family needed, but I would never take one dime from the Lords because of it. I informed him that I had told Xena about Orion and my mistake, and she promised to keep quiet for my sake.

Since the day he walked out of our office, I haven't heard a word from Orion. I battled the urge to call him but then I put myself in his shoes. What I had done was terrible. I take complete responsibility for my actions. If he never wants to see me again, then so be it. My heart still hurts. It actually aches. But I've gotten used to the feeling, which is still with me as I peruse Lonnie Blaine's audition message board.

"Oh my God," I whisper, reading the details of an audition for his latest musical. I sit up and cross my legs. I can do this. Since I haven't been going to work, I've exercised a lot. I also did a workout with

Sarah and Tab. They put complex routines together on the spot and told me to do them, and I had done them! Yesterday, they both assured me that I was ready to get back out there. And Lonnie is producing a new musical titled *Fatal Fem*.

Finally, I know what I want. There will be no more talks or thoughts of graduate school and no more inconsequential jobs that keep me from auditioning and staying in dancer's form. Without another pause, I tap the button to put my name on the audition list. Fear grips me after I complete the action. But then something else takes over me. Orion is the only reason I have easy access to Lonnie's list. I owe him a lot.

I scramble around my apartment until I find my cell phone. I have to send him a text.

At first I typed that I was sorry and hoped he was doing well. But then, I don't want him to think I'm permitting him to move on. I also don't want him to feel that I've moved on. I decide the best thing do is to keep its surface. I settle on: *Hey. What happened with Herc? Did he accept your AI software?*

My heart pounds like a broken radiator as I set my phone down on the table by the door. I do not expect him to answer me soon, if he even answers at all. But before I can turn my back on my device, it dings.

I inhale deeply when I see that I have a responding message from Orion reading: *Turned it down.*

I gasp. No wonder Orion had been extra angry at me. I knew it—Hercules shattered his self-esteem. If things hadn't gone down between us the way they had, I would've pitched him a second-option plan that I thought of. I'm excited to tell him what that plan of action was. I type: *How about Max Grove?*

That'll show Hercules.

I wait and wait, but a few minutes go by and there's no response from Orion. Maybe I insulted him, so I type: *Or not.*

He's back with: *Good idea. I'll look into it. How are you?*

I stare at the last part of his message. How am I? Trying not to miss him like crazy.

I type: *Fine. And you?*

He answers: *Fine.*

What do I say next? Should I apologize again? Yes, I should. I type: *I'm sorry for lying to you.*

With bated breath, I wait, and wait, and wait. He doesn't respond, and I'm okay with that.

On Monday morning, I'm up at the crack of dawn. Auditions start at 7:00 a.m. I scarf down two protein bars, and tepid coffee left in the carafe from the previous day and head out. I don't want to be late. Because last night it hit me, if I can't have Orion, I can at least make something out of this opportunity he gifted me. I plan on dancing my ass off today.

CHAPTER 22
I Miss Her
ORION LORD

TWO DAYS LATER

Why in the hell hadn't I thought about Max Grove sooner? I called his office on Monday; surprisingly, he took my call right then and there. I didn't beat around the bush. I told him I have artificial intelligence software he might be interested in.

He was silent for a long while.

I said, "Hello?"

"What about LTI?"

"Herc's not interested. He wouldn't even look at the demonstration."

"He never assessed the software?" Max sounded surprised by that.

"Nope."

He was silent again, but I waited. I realized thinking while silent is his style. He asked if I could give him and his team a complete demonstration on Wednesday. Then he asked an interesting question.

"Hercules doesn't take you seriously, does he?"

I swallowed hard, hoping the truth wouldn't make him change his mind. "No, he doesn't."

"But he's got good instincts," Max quickly followed up.

"That doesn't make him right about me. The thing about family is it's hard to rise above what they want you to be, need you to be."

"Ha," Max said, then quickly followed up with, "See you Wednesday."

And now I'm here. Since I've put some space between Lila and myself, I've been figuring things out myself and getting clarity about the strength of my team's AI software. I've also been giving my relationship with Lila a lot of thought. I'm talking about the relationship we had before we hooked up. Shit, I used to have her break my dates and lie to women for me. Hell, I wouldn't want to wake up believing I was married to me either.

But first things first....

Max Grove has pulled out all the stops in anticipation of my arrival. I didn't come alone. I brought Dan, Hyun, and Vic. We are each pitching different product ideas for various business sectors. I have mental health. Hyun takes entertainment. Vic is pitching education. Dan takes transportation. One by one my team members kill it. Not once has Max Grove's attention strayed. I can tell by the energy in the way he's sitting and that lively look in his eyes that he's in.

Two hours later Max asks to speak to me alone. I nod sharply and say, "Certainly."

NOW THAT WE'RE SETTLED IN A SEATING AREA IN HIS office, he asks, "Your brother turned this down?"

I sit up straighter, proud to say, "Yes, he did."

"You know what this can do for TRANSPOT? We own half the rights to that software too. You're handing me the ability to out-develop your family's company by the end of the year. Are you okay with that?" He watches me curiously.

I want to give him no doubt as I say, "He had

his chance. Plus," I crack a smile. "Aren't we all becoming one big happy family anyway?"

Max keeps a straight face, which makes me uncomfortable. I hope I haven't tanked this deal. And I think I had until he shifts abruptly, taps thoughtfully on his desk, and says, "And I like what you said about sentience. It's a waste of time. I always knew it. If the best Artificial Intelligence can be is human, then what the hell is it good for?" Finally, he smiles.

"I agree," I say and then admit Delilah was the one who steered me away from sentience.

I know we're getting somewhere when Max explains where they are with TRANSPOT, which is tele-image technology that allows users to interact through solidified light-projected images of themselves. For instance, if, say, five users are interacting in a capsule, each of those five users can interact with those five users in each user's personal space. Early trials have gone as far as to allow couples to sleep together while apart. He says his parents, Heartly and Xander Grove, use TRANSPORT often when one or the other is away from home. After clearing the lengthy government approval process, the software will revolutionize the world. But TRANSPOT can also formulate computer-generated human images that appear authentically human and that's where our AI will reign supreme.

I'm on the edge of my seat when I say, "TRANSPOT and our AI will allow fallible humans to interact with infallible machines."

"Yes," Max replies as if what I said has taken his breath away. "Let's partner."

I stand up, hand outstretched. Max stands too. It's the first time I've noticed we're the same height. The guy looks like his mother too. I never really paid much attention to him until I needed him. That's not good. I'm changing that about myself.

I'm going to change a lot about myself, and I know what to do first.

CHAPTER 23

Life Is Good

DELILAH O'SHAY

"Look who I ran into," I say.

Xena, who opens my oven and takes out baked bread, nearly drools as she stares with stars in her eyes at Lynx Grove.

Lynx is carrying my grocery bags for me. Cooking at my place is something Xena and I decided to do more often since we're so good at whipping up meals together. But this won't last long because starting Monday I'll be practicing in a new musical directed by Lonnie Blaine. I'm even playing a central supporting character, which was news to me since I auditioned for one of the unnamed character spots. Frankly, I would've taken whatever they saddled me with. But Lonnie had said that my dancing was magical and that I had a presence about me. *Wow, I'm still on cloud nine about that compliment.*

"I told Lynx he could join us for dinner. He was going to order takeout," I say.

"Oh," Xena says as if what I said was so intriguing. She's really out of sorts.

"Don't get your panties in a bunch, Zee. He's just a man," I say.

"Ha, ha, ha," Xena says teasingly.

Lynx sets the grocery bag on the counter and then rolls his sleeves up. "How can I help? I want to help."

We're making shrimp creole, so we task him with deveining the shrimp.

"Mr. Eleventh Floor, did Lilly tell you that she landed a big role in Lonnie Blaine's new musical, *Fatal Fem.*"

"No," he says all excitedly. "By the way, I'm cool with being referred to as Mr. Eleventh Floor." Both Xena and I momentarily swoon over that winning smile of his.

"It really should be illegal to be as good-looking as you are. I mean, look at him, Lilly. My panties are drenched. And I'm actually going to go do something about that. Yes, I keep a clean change of underwear in my cousin's apartment."

I gasp in shock. Xena is never that forward with guys, which is why I'm about to explain that she's had too much of her special brew of rum and wine and not enough to eat. That's why we baked bread right away. Also, since washer/dryer combos are hard to come by in New York City, she comes over to wash a lot, which is why she has panties and other articles of clothing in my apartment. But the doorbell rings and Xena treks off down the hallway before I can explain. However, I'm relieved Lynx laughs as he looks off after Xena. Who knows, they might end up making a love connection because Xena is very sexy.

"I'll be back," I say to him as I head off to see who's at my door. Out of habit I look through the peephole and gasp. "Orion?"

He waves as if he can see through the wood.

I turn to Lynx who raises his eyebrows as he's still working on the shrimp.

I take a breath to center myself and then undo the locks. My tear ducts constrict after I open the door and stand face-to-face with him.

"Hi," he says, smiling at me with glossy eyes.

"Hi."

"Can I come in?"

I glance over at Lynx, and Orion leans across

the threshold, frowning as he looks at what's captured my attention.

"Oh," he groans, tossing his head back. "Really?"

"What did you tell your cousin, Lilly?" Lynx asks. "Don't get your panties in a bunch, Orion. We're just having dinner."

First of all, when Orion leaned in close that giddy energy his nearness stirs inside me was back with a vengeance. He smells like heaven and looks like my forever.

"Orion?" Xena says, bolting into the front of the apartment and looking our way.

On that note, I guide him into the hallway and close the door behind us.

Now that we're alone, we're grinning at each other.

"You've got quite a guest list inside," he says.

"Are you joining us?" My heart is beating like crazy.

"Are you asking me to stay?"

"I am."

It happens so fast. I'm in his powerful arms and his body is pressed against mine.

"Maybe," he whispers.

The corners of my mouth pull down from disappointment.

"I followed your advice and contacted Max Grove."

My eyebrows shoot up. "Oh… What happened?"

His smile's even bigger. "I'll be working with him."

"Good. That's really good." I feel so happy for him. "Oh, and I'm dancing in a new musical. I was cast by Lonnie Blaine—thank you for the opportunity."

"Good," he says.

"And I'm sorry," I say as if out of breath.

"Babe, you don't have to apologize again. Your apology is accepted."

I feel it…

It's as if for the past uncountable days, my body has been holding its breath and finally, it lets out out sigh and relaxes.

"I love you," he whispers. His voice is thick and emotional.

"I love you too."

His arms wrap around me. My body merges with his, and his tongue swirls around mine. As we kiss, I feel like I'm floating to another planet.

"Hey, wife," he says when our lips part.

I chuckle. "Hey, husband."

"I don't want to be apart from you," he whispers.

I brush the side of his face with the backs of my fingers. "Okay," I whisper back.

That naughty look that I love comes to Orion's eyes. "Then come with me."

I quickly glance over my shoulder and at the door. "What? I have guests. And no shoes on."

"They'll be fine and you don't need shoes because you're going to be in my bed."

I stretch my bottom lip squeamishly as I think. Xena is going to kill me. Or…maybe not. She'll be alone with Lynx. I wonder what she would do with the opportunity.

I narrow an eye impishly. "Okay. Let's go."

"Yeah?" He seems surprised.

"Yeah."

In one sweep of his strong arms, Orion lifts my feet off the carpet and cradles me in his arms. We kiss, my head spins, and my sex weeps for him as he carries me to the elevator.

Epilogue

DELILAH O'SHAY

TWO MONTHS AFTER THE TWO MONTHS' NOTICE

We set the timer and now sit on the foot of our humungous bed. Yes, I live with Orion now, and our penthouse has bells and whistles that I've only seen on lifestyles of the ultra-rich programs. We have a full-time maid and chef. Once I tried making our bed, the maids came behind me and remade it. And our bathroom... That's where I spend the most time when I'm home. I take a lot of warm baths. Sometimes, if he's home, Orion will join me. And guess what happens when he joins me? That's why we're home today at 2:33 p.m. He's usually at the office working on perfecting and creating products for his AI software. I'm generally at rehearsal at this time of day.

I did try to go to practice today. The play starts in less than thirty days, but I struggled so much to get through today's scene, which required a physically demanding dance number, that I had to stop and ask to go home. Who am I kidding? My nipples are so tender that a feather brushing over them can make me wince. My pee is the color of mustard. And if I even get a whiff of bell peppers, I want to hurl. Also, my period is a week late, and it's not even hinting that it might come real soon.

"How long do we have to wait?" Orion asks.

"Fifteen minutes," I say with a sigh.

He drums the front of the bed. There's excitement in the pitter-patter sound that his hands just made. He's happy. I'm sort of happy too. The thing is, I'll have to quit the show after I've just been moved up to the lead role. Kelly, who played Zara, the main female heroine, had to back out because she was pregnant. There's something about that role. Whoever gets it next might be pregnant too. But…the jury is still out. I might have a hormonal imbalance from long rehearsals and an abrupt change in my diet, which is healthier than before.

"From married to having a baby in four months," Orion says and then chuckles.

I raise a finger in objection. "We don't know if we're having a baby yet."

"Babe...come on."

I close my eyes tightly. "I know. But still, we can have hope."

"I'm okay with it," he quickly says. "I always wanted to be a dad. I'd be a good dad. And look, I've been a good husband. You gotta give me points for that."

Chuckling, I rub my hand up and down his solid stone body. Orion's body still feels like it's made of marble. Gosh, I love when he wraps me up in bed. I love sleeping against him. "You have been a husband above all husbands."

We turn to face each other simultaneously, and our lips indulge in sensual kissing.

"Umm," I moan as my head feels like it wants to float.

"You're wearing your leotard," he says between kisses.

"Um-hum," I purr.

Earlier, I asked Ellis to take me to the drugstore

after I left practice, and I bought three brands of pregnancy tests. On the way home, I called Orion and told him what I planned to do.

"I'm on my way," he had said. And now here we are.

"It's the kind that snaps open," he says—*or is he asking?*

"Um-hum," I say.

Orion nods thoughtfully. "Can we, um, do it?"

I tilt my head, eyeing him inquisitively. "Do it? Or Do *it?*"

He raises his eyebrows. "Do *it.*"

I can't stop smirking at him as I slowly rise to my feet and then hold my hand out for him to take.

Orion swallows as he intensifies our eye contact.

Standing face to face, I grab hold of his strong shoulders, perfect my balance and then gradually raise my leg.

"Ooh..." He sighs as if he can hardly contain himself.

My ankle rests on his shoulder, and he draws me against him. Orion sniffs my skin as his finger softly slides up and down the crotch of my leotard. The challenge for me is to stay standing while he...

"Ha," I gasp after he pulls open the clasps of my leotard and starts immediately stimulating me.

My grounding leg shakes as I wrap my arms around his neck.

"Yes, baby," he whispers. "I love you, Lila."

I open my eyes when he says that. Our gazes are so connected that I feel like I'm falling into him. "I love you too."

Our breaths crash against each other. "I loved you longer," he says.

"I know," I strain to say.

He told me he's been in love with me since weeks after he hired me. He didn't think he was good enough. But after he read my two-weeks notice, he decided to make a play for me.

My orgasm is blooming, and I have difficulty standing on one leg. And as part of the routine we've perfected, Orion grips me by the calve, guides me down on the bed, and now my clit is stimulated by his warm and soft mouth.

"O…" I shudder as I grasp two handfuls of our duvet as my orgasm expands, expands, and then…

"Ha!" I cry out as my sex pulses long enough for Orion to unzip and free himself. I gasp when he thrusts himself inside me.

THE ALARM IS RINGING, BUT ORION IS PUMPING slowly and indulgently in and out of me. We haven't looked away from each other because we can't. I love seeing all the expressions his face makes when we make love. He enjoys this so much, and so do I.

"If it's positive," he says breathlessly. "We're going to have a party, baby."

His thrusting feels so good; I'm about to come. All I can do is try to nod.

"I want you to be happy about this. Are you happy?" he asks.

My mouth falls open. I hate that I had given him the impression that I'm not over the moon about the possibility of carrying our child. Sure, I'll have to give up the lead role in *Fatal Fem*. But that's fine. There will be more roles. But there's only one Orion and only one of our maybe baby, and both are worth more to me than anything in the world. "Very," I whimper.

"Good," he says, and then, "You first."

He wants me to come first, and he expertly makes it happen.

AFTER I CLIMAX, THEN HE CLIMAXES. FINALLY, WE raise our eyebrows, nod, then race to the bathroom as fast as we can.

Orion has the stick in his hand, reading it.

"What does it say?" I ask.

His expression falls, and my heart constricts. Then, he smiles as big as the earth and says, "We're having a baby, baby!"

I nudge him for his little joke, and then we hug tightly. Who would've ever guessed that I would end up happily in love, married, and having a baby with the boss I thought I hated so much.

Made in the USA
Las Vegas, NV
31 October 2022